C That's Why I Don't Fool with Women Part 1

This is a work of fiction and, as such, it is a product of the author's creative imagination. All name of characters, organizations, and events portrayed in the novel are fictitious. Any similarities of the characters to real persons, whether living or dead, or coincidental. Any resemblance of incidents portrayed in this book to actual events, is likewise coincidental.

Copyright 2018 by Sherre Still. Published by Still Making It

All rights and reserved. Printed in the United States of America.

ISBN 978-0-578-21223-4

ISBN -978-0-578-21224-1

Dedication

To my grandma Mary-Lee, who's been gone three years—may your soul rest in peace. I wish you were here to share this special moment with me once this book is published. RIP to my dear brother and dear friend Dilbert Madison (Doe-Doe) We miss you so much.

To my family—for your support through my down period and seeing me come back up yet again. Thank you to my graphic designer Mr. Reese Barnett, Mrs. Halima Martin my photographer, and my girl

Mrs. Deanne Williams. And finally thank you to my beautiful models on the book cover y'all struck a pose honey yes

Sherre Still

It was a cold winter day when Ree thought it would be nice to surprise her grandmother Mary-Lee with lunch. It was Ree's day off work as a registered nurse at the hospital, and she figured that she would visit her grandmother since she had been promising to visit and had never gotten around to it. Ree got out of her car with the food, trying her best to rush out of the cold and into the senior citizen apartment building where her grandmother lived. There was no one at the door to let her in, so she rang the bell outside of the management office and shivered as she waited for someone to open it. *Damn, I wish someone would hurry up and answer the intercom or see me standing out here. If they don't, I'm going to have to buzz grandma's button and I wanted to surprise her,* Ree thought.

"May I help you?" the office manager asked through the intercom.

"Hey, Ms. Needest! This is Ree, Ms. Mary-Lee's granddaughter. Can you buzz me in?" Ree asked while turning her face away from the cold wind that was blowing in her face.

Without answering the question, Ms. Needest buzzed Ree in.

Ree signed in and joined a resident on the elevator who had been sitting in the lobby the whole time. "Who are you here to see?" the resident asked. Ree ignored the question. *Where the fuck were you when I was trying to get in this building? Had you let me in, I would have happily told you who I came to visit,* Ree thought.

The elevator stopped on the fifth floor and Ree got off and headed to her grandma's apartment. She prepared herself for the good laugh that was to come. She heard the TV blaring and knocked on her grandmother's door. When there was no answer, she knocked again. She wondered if her grandmother was taking a nap. When her grandmother still didn't answer, Ree feared something was wrong. Her grandmother mentioned not feeling great the night before. Ree called the management office to open the door. Ms. Needest came up right away, because there had been three deaths in the building in the past week. When Ms. Needest put the key in the door, Ree heard something sliding from the door. Then the door opened quickly.

C' That's Why I Don't Fool with Women

"Grandma, I thought something was wrong, so I called Ms. Needest to let me in so that we could check on you. Why didn't you answer when I knocked on the door?" Ree asked while laughing at her grandmother holding a butcher knife in her hand like she was ready to cut somebody. Ms. Needest just walked away laughing, relieved to see Ms. Mary-Lee was alive, because she knew that she could be a handful.

"I didn't answer the door because I thought you were one of these residents coming to beg for a cup of sugar or a stick of butter. Your Uncle Duck took me to the grocery store the other day and a few people that live on my floor were just eye balling my groceries, so they could knock on my door and know what to ask for. Come on in here, because someone is probably looking through their peephole at us or got their ear to their door trying to listen to what the hell I'm saying," Mary-Lee said, stepping aside so that her granddaughter could walk in.

"Grandma, you are a mess," Ree said laughing as she went in her grandmother's apartment. Ree walked inside her grandmother's one-bedroom apartment and thought she was going to die from heat. It had to be at least 110 degrees in there. Ree looked around and could see her grandma had all four burners of the electric stove on and the oven set to 200 degrees. The thermostat was on 70. Grandma Mary-Lee sat down on the couch in her grandma panties and bra. She called that her comfortable wardrobe.

"What you got in that bag girl?" Grandma Mary-Lee asked.

"I brought lunch over for us grandma, but I need for you to do me a favor. Turn the stove off and put some clothes on. I'm going to pass out in here,"

Mary-Lee went to get a duster robe and a pair of house shoes to put on while Ree turned the stove off and warmed up the soup and sandwiches in the microwave.

"Did you bring me a can of soda to go along with our lunch, Ree?" Mary-Lee asked.

"No granny, I didn't bring any soda but drinking water ain't bad for the body," Ree said while waiting on the food to heat up in the microwave.

Sherre Still

Mary-Lee got up from the table and went to her bedroom. She came back moments later fully dressed in a polyester button-down shirt with elastic around the waist and polyester bell bottom pants. *I see where Uncle Duck gets his sense of style,* Ree thought.

"Come on child! You of all people know I don't play about my soda when I'm eating my food," Mary-Lee said, locking her apartment door with Ree standing beside her.

All Ree could do was laugh at her grandmother, who was still in her right mind at 90 years old.

They got off the elevator and passed a group of women playing cards in the lobby.

"Hey Mary-Lee," one of the residents said.

"Hey to you," Mary-Lee said. "Keep on walking child, and don't talk to these women," she whispered to Ree. They headed toward the vending machine, and one of the residents followed them.

"Mary-Lee, ah I was wondering if you would mind lending me a stick of butter and a cup of instant coffee," the resident said.

Oh shit! Grandma is going to go the fuck off on this lady, Ree thought. Mary-Lee stopped putting coins in the vending machine and handed the rest of the coins to Ree as she turned to address the resident. "Listen here, now it's the beginning of the damn month, and I know your birthdate because it was in the monthly announcements. I don't lend shit, so I suggest you use your food stamps wisely, so you won't have to ask anybody for nothing," Mary-Lee said with a bunch of attitude.

Damn, people their age still go through bullshit like this hanging with a group of women that talk behind your back and then will come grinning in your face begging for stuff, Ree thought. The resident walked away without saying a word. She just gave Mary-Lee a dirty look before getting out of her sight. By the time Ree and her grandmother made it to the lobby to get on the elevator, Ms. Needest was waiting patiently.

"Ms. Mary-Lee can I speak with you privately in my office?" Ms. Needest asked, not wanting to make it obvious that one of the four ladies playing cards had reported something to her. Ree stayed behind just to

C' That's Why I Don't Fool with Women

look at the four women playing cards until her grandmother returned. It took no more than 10 minutes for Mary-Lee to return to the lobby looking like she was ready to kick some old folks' ass.

"See, that's why I don't fool with women. They can be so damn chatty and full of a bunch of bullshit," Mary-Lee said as Ree gently grabbed her hand and escorted her to the elevator. The four women kept playing cards until the elevator door closed.

"You better watch your back, Shanandoah. If Mary-Lee finds out, you were the one that told Ms. Needest she had on house shoes down here it's going to be trouble for you. I heard the old bitch can be a real pistol whip when fighting," one of the residents said.

Mary-Lee was in an altercation within a week of moving into the building after being accused of flirting with somebody's husband. Two of the women decided to call it a day because they feared Mary-Lee was going to come back downstairs to start some trouble. Trying her best to calm her grandmother down, Ree told her grandmother that confronting the gossipers wasn't worth being put out of the building. Mary-Lee had lived with Ree's mother and then with her son Duck and his wife and Buck-Lu and his wife. None of those living arrangements worked out. Mary-Lee knew Ree was telling the truth, so she went back to her apartment.

"Look Ree, I told you these people are so damn nosey and greedy. I bought real damn butter, not margarine, so that lady knew what to ask for," Mary-Lee said.

Ree ushered her grandmother to sit down at the table so they could enjoy the lunch and not focus on the drama other people were trying to cause. "So how do you like the cream of broccoli soup and the meatball sandwich, grandma?" Ree asked.

"It's really good. I'm glad you didn't get something that I know I couldn't really eat. Then I'd have to lie and say that I enjoyed it. It is hard to eat without having your natural teeth in your mouth, so you better take damn good care of yours because by the time you retire ain't no telling what kind of insurance you're going to have even though you work, honey child. Back in the day, I remember if you didn't have a job Medicaid health insurance covered vision, dental and health. Now you must be half dead just to get health insurance. Yo Uncle Duck say he's going to buy me another pair of dentures, but I told him not to waste any more money on me because I don't have too much time on this earth. The new dentures hurt my gums, and I don't like strange people asking me to open wide when playing with my mouth to get measurements,"

Ree was glad now that she surprised her grandmother for the visit, because to hear her say that she didn't have long on this earth might be a sign that she is ready to meet her maker and live with God. Ree left the table to wash her hands and wipe a tear from her eye.

"Grandma," Ree said, shedding another tear.

"Yeah baby what is it? What's wrong?" Mary-Lee asked.

"I want you to know that I love you, and I never want you to forget that ever," Ree said.

"Hell, girl I know that you love me. You are one out of 20 of the grandchildren I have that visits me wherever I'm living and spends quality time with me. Don't shed another tear for me, Ree. I'm going to tell you why, baby. I've had my fun. If I have no damn more at 90 years old and can remember everything I did then I'm in good shape. Do you hear what I say now?" Mary-Lee asked as she hugged her granddaughter tight. She didn't want to let her go because she knew Ree was getting ready to leave.

"Yeah grandma I know what you mean," Ree said laughing and trying not to think about her grandmother ever leaving this world.

"When are you coming back to visit me Ms. Working Lady?" Mary-Lee asked her granddaughter.

"I'll come by sometime next week," Ree said as she told her grandmother she needed to get going. Silently watching her grandmother, Ree put on her jacket and put her purse over her shoulder. She walked over to her grandmother to hug and kiss her once more before leaving. "I love you grandma,".

"Grandma loves you too,"

When Ree got off the elevator, Ms. Shanandoah stopped her, because she didn't want any trouble for the shit she had started with her grandmother. "Excuse me, sweetheart," Ms. Shanandoah said to get Ree's attention.

C' That's Why I Don't Fool with Women

"Yes ma'am," Ree said, turning around to acknowledge her.

"Will you please tell your grandmother that I wasn't trying to get her in trouble by telling Ms. Needest that she had on house shoes down here in the lobby? We can't wear house shoes down here because you can fall getting on or off the elevator so that's why I told Ms. Needest, sweetheart. Can you please let your grandmother know I meant no harm toward her? Ms. Shanandoah asked, hoping to make peace.

"Ma'am, I would say that it would be better if my grandmother didn't find out that you were the one that told Ms. Needest anything, because if I tell her what you said she is going to certainly knock on your door, and it ain't going to be anything I'm going to be able to do about that," Ree said before leaving.

When Ree got in her car to start the engine to warm up, she could see her grandmother waving at her from her apartment window. Ree's cellphone rang. It was Mary-Lee calling. "Yes, grandma, I'm in the car safe and the doors are locked" Ree said.

"What took you so doggone long to get in your car, baby?" Mary-Lee asked.

"I was looking for my car keys in the lobby so that I wouldn't have to stand in the cold and freeze trying to unlock the car door," Ree lied for a good reason.

"Well call me once you get home. I love you, child. Now get off the parking lot and drive because that's a fancy car you are driving in this kind of neighborhood,".

"Ok, I'm getting ready to drive off now grandma. Bye,".

"Ah you need to say my long-time saying baby,".

"Oh yeah, C that's why I don't fool with women," they both said laughing before ending their conversation.

Sherre Still

I Completely Forgot I was off for the Weekend

I don't know what to do with myself having a three-day stretch off from work, Ree thought to herself as she rolled over in bed thinking of her visit with her grandmother the day before. Ree's hubby was out of town on business and there were no kids to take care of, so Ree had plenty of damn time on her hands to do whatever she pleased. *Let me call a few of my girlfriends and see what I can get into later tonight,* Ree thought as she called one of her dearest friends. The telephone rang a few times before her friend picked up.

"Hello," Ila answered.

"Hey, what's up, girlfriend," Ree said, happy her friend answered the telephone.

Ila had to look at the telephone before speaking to make sure she was really talking to Ree, who had been missing in action at most of the girlfriend gatherings. "Is this the real Ree calling me who works all of the damn time and has no time for her friend's, bitch?" Ila asked.

All Ree could do was laugh, because it was true that she had been working like a Hebrew slave, but she knew her priorities; friends

C' That's Why I Don't Fool with Women

weren't top priority. She needed to make some money. "Yes bitch, it's me, the real Ree. Guess who is off work and have free to play all day without her hubby being at home?" Ree asked.

"Aw hell naw bitch! You want to come hang out with the girls because you ain't got shit to do because your husband is out of town on another one of his business trips with a hoe," Ila said laughing.

"Ha ha ha bitch. Now stop playing before our conversation becomes real serious, bitch," Ree said, meaning every word that came out of her mouth. Ree didn't kid around about her parents and her man. She'd feel the same way about her kids if she had any.

Ila stopped laughing and apologized because she knew Ree was pissed off. Ila was just kidding around. "So, what you want to get into Ree? You're lucky that Hampton has a bachelor party to go to tonight. I was just going to catch a movie or something and go out for dinner," Ila said.

"I was thinking more on the line of shaking the booty that my momma blessed me with in the club if you know what I mean. It ain't too often I get to go out to the club without being questioned when I come in the house if you know what I'm saying," Ree said.

I know what you mean. You don't want Falcon kicking your ass, because he knows how you act when you're not in his presence, Ila thought. "I'm down for the club if that's what you want to do. Around what time you want to meet up and go?" Ila asked so that she could go to the beauty shop and get her hair done.

"I say that we go out around 9:30 tonight so that we can have a place to sit and be by the dance floor," Ree suggested. So, it was a date night for the girls' night out. Once Ree got off the telephone, she went to her closet to find an outfit. *Should I wear high heels or flats, so I can really get down on the dance floor,* Ree thought as she danced in her walk-in closet. The ringing telephone broke Ree's concentration. "Hello," Ree said as though she had an attitude.

"What's going on there, Ree? Why are you sounding like that? Is everything ok?" Falcon asked out of concern.

"Oh, I was doing some paperwork and got distracted when the telephone rang. That's all, baby," Ree lied because she knew her husband wouldn't appreciate hearing she was going out with some of her friends to shake her ass in the club. How's the convention going?" Ree asked.

"Things here are a bit hectic, but yo man can handle the business that's thrown at him,".

"That's right, baby. Talk that talk," The Street's both laughed and said that they loved each other before getting off the telephone. Ree went back to looking for something to wear for her night out on the town.

C' That's Why I Don't Fool with Women

Saturday Night Out

When Ree arrived at Ila's home, she couldn't believe that she was waiting on her friend to finish getting dressed at 10:30 p.m. *I should have gone out by my damn self. Ila's ass has changed at least five different times since I've been here, and if she changes one more time I'm going to leave her ass behind*, Ree thought.

"I'm ready, Ree. Let's go and party hardy," Ila said with Ree walking behind her a bit upset.

"Ila you're driving because you weren't ready when I came to pick you up, changing clothes a hundred times," Ree said. It was nothing for Ila to pop the locks to her sport Corvette so Ree could shut the fuck up and sit in the passenger seat. Sipping some liquor from her flask, Ree wanted to get her buzz on before arriving at the club and spending $14 on a drink.

Sherre Still

Ila parked in the V.I.P. section where she normally parked at Plural nightclub. She looked over at her friend. "You ready to kick it or what?" she asked.

Ree was from the Show Me state. She politely got out of the car and walked toward the club dancing with Ila laughing and following behind her, letting her know she was ready to kick it. It cost $15 to get in the club. Ree pulled out her money, but Ila walked right in, telling Ree to come on and put her wallet away. *Shit, it's been a long time since I've been out to know Ila got some clout,* Ree thought as she walked inside of the club for free.

Ila looked around until she found her friends. "Hey y'all," she said as she danced standing beside the table where her friends were sitting.

Ain't this some shit, Ree thought as she looked at Sharia, Zantaneek and Del'Feela. None of the women were fond of Ree. The women were looking at Ree the same way, thinking, *who invited this bitch? I thought she fell off the planet Earth, because Ila hadn't been mentioning her name.*

I'm not going to allow these heffas to steal my girl's night out, Ree thought as she went to the dance floor when a gentleman asked her to dance. "Isn't Ree still married?" Del'Feela asked the other ladies as they all looked at Ila and Ree's hands to check for wedding rings.

When Ila came back to the table, the conversation stopped. "Woo the DJ is playing some good music tonight," Ila said, still popping her fingers to the beat and wiping sweat from her forehead.

"Hey Ila, is Ree still married?" Sharia asked. The curiosity was killing her.

"Ah yes, Ree is still married. Why are you asking about her personal business?" Ila asked, peeping that someone was being nosey. Sharia

C' That's Why I Don't Fool with Women

tried to play dumb by saying that she was going to try and hook Ree up with her brother. Ila knew Sharia was lying about trying to make a love connection, because her brother had never been interested in women. When Ree came back to the table and saw the hags staring at her with fake smiles, she sat beside Ila to keep from making conversation with the enemies for the hell of it. The gentleman that Ree was dancing with brought the waitress over with him to the table where Ree was sitting to ask if he could buy her and her friends a drink. Del-Feela, Sharia and Zantaneek hurried drinking their watered downed drinks with preparation to order something they would never order because it was going to be free. Ree had peeped game and played things cool. She politely told the waitress what she and Ila drank and then thanked the gentleman for thinking of her. Zantaneek, Del'Feela and Sharia were pissed off because a complimentary drink wasn't ordered for them. Once the drinks were served, Ree and Ila toasted to one another, drank and then went back to the dance floor to keep the party going.

"Them bitches," Del'Feela said as soon as Ila and Ree went on the dance floor.

Zantaneek wanted so badly for any man to ask her to dance but no dude was looking her way. Del'Feela went to the dance floor to dance by herself. She refused to sit and watch Ree and Ila have a good time and not enjoy herself. Feeling strange because no one came to join her while she was doing her thang, Del'Feela went to sit her fat ass back down. *That's what her big ass gets*, Sharia and Zantneek thought as Del'Feela came walking their way. Ila's feet began to hurt so she went back to sit with her other girlfriends who were mad that she had invited Ree to hang out with them. *That hoe is ungrateful to have a husband and in here dancing up close with another man that she hasn't promised herself to until she dies. What a shame*, Zantaneek thought as she watched Ree smile at her from the dance floor.

The gentleman didn't want to let Ree out of his sight without at least getting her telephone number, so they could talk from time to time. "My name is Cooper but my friend's call me Coop. I would like to get your telephone number if you don't mind," he said.

"Coop, I'm a married woman out here having a good time for tonight only while my husband is away. Go to the bar baby and take a load off of your feet. There's a drink for you once you sit down," Ree said, moving across the dance floor to dance with another dude she knew from back in her single to mingle days that was fanning her his way. Ree had prepaid for Cooper's drink when he bought Ila and her a drink, showing that she could return the favor. Cooper went to the bar to find out if Ree was telling the truth and sure enough the bartender asked him what he was drinking compliments of the lady on the dance floor in the red dress. Shaking his head and sipping his drink, Cooper liked Ree even more for her honesty about being married and being nice by returning the favor instead of taking advantage like many other sistas would.

Zantaneek, Sharia and Del'Feela had left the club because they were overdressed, and no one was buying them drinks or asking them to dance. Ree was now ready to take a shower and get under the covers to sleep like a baby after staying up past her bedtime. Ila, on the other hand, wanted to stay and continue to talk to someone she was really vibing with since the other girlfriends had gone home and weren't around to monitor her behavior.

C' That's Why I Don't Fool with Women

Shit

Once Ree finally made it home at 5 a.m., she knew she was in trouble after hearing her voice messages from Falcon. "It took me to go out of town for you to dress like you're a single woman and not come home at a decent damn hour, Ree," Falcon said before slamming the telephone down.

Now it's going to be a long, drawn-out conversation when I talk to Falcon's ass on the telephone later today if he ain't already on a plane on his way home to confront me face-to-face, Ree thought as she took off her sweaty red dress to take a shower. Ree couldn't get out of the shower before the telephone began to ring. She knew it was Falcon. "Hello," Ree said as calmly as she could.

"Don't you mean good morning instead of saying hello?" Falcon said, about to come through the telephone.

"Who in the hell you thinking you're talking too, Fal?" Ree asked, trying to dry her body off as she talked to her husband.

When Falcon heard Ree call him by his nickname, it softened him up a bit. Ree wondered how Falcon knew what she wore and what time she got home. "I saw everything on the home security system," Falcon said pissed

She felt like Falcon had gone too far by watching her like a dog when he was away, but she figured she would have a heart-to-heart talk with him when he got home. "Fal, we need to talk once you come back home seriously, because this isn't right for you to be treating me like your child," Ree said.

"Well if you didn't act like one when I'm away then maybe I wouldn't treat you like a child," Falcon said. Ree hung up on her husband, because she was ready to go to sleep and put their conversation to rest at the same damn time.

C' That's Why I Don't Fool with Women

I Need to Lean Upon Him

Ree met up with her mother and Grandma Mary-Lee at church to get some spiritual guidance in her life because she was feeling a certain kind of way about her marriage. *Lord, it's only so much I can take. I have never once stepped outside of my marriage and committed adultery, but I'm accused of it all the time when my man isn't around. Please let Falcon return home as a loving husband and as the man I once knew or I'm moving on with my life without him*, Ree thought.

"Hey baby, you look worried. I told you not to be worried about grandma, child," Mary-Lee said, thinking Ree was still thinking of the last conversation they had when she last visited.

"No grandma, that's not on my mind. It's my marriage," Ree whispered. She didn't want her mother to hear.

Violet, Ree's mother, wasn't too fond of her son-in-law, who was old enough to be her eldest brother instead of a son. "Did that old ass nigga do something to you, Ree?" Violet asked, ready to leave church to find Falcon.

"No momma, Falcon has never put a hand on me. He's just so possessive when he's not around, but let's talk about it later so the entire church won't spread my business around town," Ree whispered before the pastor preached the sermon.

Violet couldn't think straight knowing that Ree was dealing with an old ass man old enough to be her father. She raised Ree to be independent, so it was a slap in the face when her daughter brought Falcon's old ass around and introduced him as her man friend instead of her boyfriend. Violet thought Ree was going through some type of change in life and just trying something out to be dating a man so damn old, but when they got engaged she knew things were truly serious. Ree met Falcon while she was doing her clinical work in nursing school, and he swept her off her feet the moment she first saw him. She didn't have a problem with him being 35 years her senior. Praising God, rejoicing and feeling the Holy Spirit, Ree felt that things were going to be alright, knowing that she had done nothing wrong toward her husband and had no reason to feel guilty.

C' That's Why I Don't Fool with Women

Ila

Hampton wasn't happy about Ila returning home after he arrived. He was the man of the house and felt like he wore the pants. "So, let's talk about you going out with the girls and walking in the house after me at 6:00 in the morning," Hampton said as he drank a can of beer.

Ila wanted to say, "Let's talk about your drinking problem," but she didn't want to get punched dead in the mouth and have her husband apologize and claim that she made him do what he did. She made sure she stayed a safe distance away from Hampton, so that she could run if she needed to. "Hampton, I told you I went out with Ree to the movies. Then we went for dinner and had a bottle of wine at her house since Falcon was out of town on business. Time just passed by and next thing we knew it was almost 5:30 this morning, not 6:00 as you claim it was when I came home. It will never happen again. I promise, baby; please forgive me. What do you want to eat for breakfast before I go to work?" Ila asked, praying that it was the end of their conversation.

Sherre Still

"It better be your last time coming in this time of morning, knowing your curfew is 1:30 a.m. I don't want anything to eat, but you should go take your ass in the bedroom and pose for me until I finish drinking my beer, and I'll be right there when I finish," Hampton said. As she was told, Ila went to the bedroom to disrobe and get in bed until Hampton came to join her.

Hampton was a well-known mechanic that had four auto mechanic shops in St. Louis. After Hampton's father died, his mom was too lazy to take over the family business, so Hampton was chosen to continue the legacy since his three brothers were addicted to drugs. Ila was a registered nurse and could easily walk away from the marriage that she had been in for eight years, but she thought there was no other man out there that could make her feel the way that asshole made her feel.

C' That's Why I Don't Fool with Women

Zantaneek

One of the wittiest people out of the bunch, Zanataneek was a bitter, divorced mother of one and didn't appreciate her career as a lawyer. Ila would tell Zantaneek all the time that she would rather run circles in the courtroom than spend the day wiping assess and passing pills, but she wasn't smart enough to pass the bar exam on the first try. Zantaneek had only lost two cases out of her whole 10-year career. One of the cases that Zantaneek lost was her own divorce, because she was too damn emotional representing herself. Her ex-husband was a judge and, unbeknownst to Zantaneek, a judge friend of his handled the case. Zantaneek didn't have a fighting chance in hell.

"Mantha get your stuff together so that you can be ready to go when your father pulls up in front of the house. He has texted me that he'll be here in 10 minutes, and I know he's bringing that stepmother of yours along," Zantaneek said, trying to plant hate in her daughter's heart.

Sherre Still

I don't know why momma is tripping and trying to put me in the middle of her shit still with hating daddy. That's between her and him. If she and daddy get me what I need, I'm cool with both of them, Mantha thought as she grabbed her overnight bag and walked toward the door.

"Bye momma, I'll see you when I get back. Love you," Mantha said, slamming the door.

Zantaneek ran to the window to get a glimpse of Bellow Clifford's wife but still didn't know what the hell she looked like after he'd been married a year. Time and time again, Zantaneek asked her daughter to at least take a picture of her step-mother so she could see what the Caucasian woman looked like, but Mantha would say she was having so much fun that she completely forgot to get a picture, which would make Zantaneek mad.

Del'Feela

A true hustler, Del'Feela had many struggles. She couldn't understand why she couldn't meet the man of her dreams and just live the life that she wanted to live. Feeling like things couldn't possibly get any worst, Del'Feela felt obligated to take care of her ill mother, who seemed to be aging fast.

Sherre Still

Sharia

Sharia was a housewife who wished she had gotten her career before the husband and four kids. Feeling cheated out of happiness, Sharia would look at her friends' lives thinking that they all had it going on because they had money in the bank and a lot of material things to match. Sharia felt like all her fun stopped the moment she got married. On Sharia and Wentzville's wedding day, the church basement flooded where the reception was going to be held. The best man pawned Sharia's wedding ring. Wentzville's mother pretended to be ill to keep from attending the wedding. With the babies coming back to back each year after marriage, Sharia thought she would never get a break after birthing four children. She demanded that her husband sign paperwork permitting her to get her tubes tied. If he refused, she was going to ask for a divorce. After losing weight and getting her hour glass shape back, Sharia was less depressed and a little happier when being out in her community mingling with her girlfriends once again.

C' That's Why I Don't Fool with Women

Confronting the Issue

When Falcon arrived home, he was more than ready to talk since Ree hung up in his ear and he had time to think of how he had approached her. Seeing the shadow of her husband standing in the doorway of the bedroom, Ree sat up in the bed to pleasantly greet her man. "Hey Fal, how was your flight?" she asked as though they never had the argument over the telephone.

"My flight is not what I want to talk about, Ree. I want to address you hanging up in my ear when I was still talking to you," Falcon said, breathing his breath in her face. This was something new Falcon was now doing, which was meant to plant fear in his young wife's heart. But oh, Falcon was sadly mistaking his wife for being a woman who was easily intimidated. Ree grabbed the telephone and threw it as Falcon reached to grab her around the neck. Missing Ree's neck, Falcon tried reaching again and Ree hit him in the head with the telephone. "You're trying to kill me after all I've done for you?" Falcon asked, holding his head in pain.

    Ree didn't answer. She was calling the police on Falcon's old ass before she murdered her husband for real. Ree's mom taught her that if a man hit you once, he would do it again and she wasn't having that in her life. After telling the police that she wanted to report an assault, Ree got out of bed still holding the telephone just in case she had to hit Falcon in the head again if he ran up on her. When the police arrived, Falcon tried to reason with the Caucasian officers, stating that it was clearly a misunderstanding. Falcon felt bad about being a jealous man running high off his emotions, but he just couldn't help himself being married to such a beautiful young woman. After Ree watched the cops put Falcon in handcuffs and put him in the back of the police car, she started packing her clothes. Zantaneek's ex-husband was a judge and Falcon's golf buddy, so Ree knew he would have Falcon out of jail in a couple of hours. *The nerve of that bastard to try to even think about choking me,* Ree thought as she cried and packed her belongings.

    She filled up her car with all she could take and looked at the house that wasn't a home to her anymore as she drove away. Ree knew that she would have to come up with a damn good lie when she arrived at her mother's home to stay for a couple of days, because Violet would be livid if she knew Falcon tried to hit Ree.

C' That's Why I Don't Fool with Women

Really Feeling Bad

   Sitting behind bars, Falcon wished like hell he was still out of town at the doctor's convention and could start over with Ree. "Damn, damn, damn," Falcon said in a low voice until he heard the officer call his name. Falcon walked over to the bars looking like a lost puppy to find out why his name was called. "Your bail has been posted. C'mon so that you can get your personal belongings," the officer said. Falcon hurried up and stepped out of the cell, because he didn't want to spend another minute with the young hoodlums that were threating to take his shoes. Relieved to see a recognizable face, Falcon gave Bellow some dap, happy he was able to come to his rescue.

   Getting straight to the point when they got in the car, the judge questioned his golf buddy.
   "So, tell me what the hell happened Falcon. My wife called me stating it was an emergency and that you were locked up. I was like where in the hell did you say he's at again? I knew I had to come and get you out

of the jam you were in, because you would have been locked up for at least two days," Bellow said.

"Well Judge Bellow, I appreciate you being my friend and coming as soon as you could to get me out of jail. Ree and I had a disagreement and things got out of control. I pray that Ree hasn't left me for good, because we never fought in the 10 years we've been married," Falcon said, feeling remorseful.

Bellow had been in Falcon's position and knew where he was coming from, so he gave him some wise advice, hoping that his friend took heed. "Well, I'm going to suggest you keep the wife if you have a chance to make the relationship work because it's cheaper to keep Ree in your life. Trust me man. When Zantaneek and I separated, it was ugly she received the news of my engagement to my current wife it got even worse. Life was hell for about six months after that. I had to get a restraining order on Zantaneek to make her stop the bullshit before I had to hire a hit man to kill the bitch. She didn't want anybody to find out she had a restraining order attached to her name, so she stopped the bull crap," Bellow said as he drove his friend home.

Falcon sat in the passenger seat listening to all the advice and prayed that there was still a great chance for his marriage. Once at home, Falcon thanked Bellow for the advice and got out of the car. Slowly, Falcon walked up the steps to his house, preparing to say he was truly sorry for what he said and was about to do out of jealousy. Unlocking the door slowly, Falcon was hoping Ree hadn't gone to work so they could talk and then possibly make love. "Ree," Falcon said as he walked down the hallway looking in each room. Mad at himself, Falcon sat down on his bed and glanced in Ree's walk-in closet, finding that most of her belongings were gone.

C' That's Why I Don't Fool with Women

Mother's Knows Best Most of the Time

"I warned that old bastard that if he ev'va did anything to hurt your feelings he would definitely have to answer to me," Violet said while puffing on her cigarette. Ree hated that she even told her mom that she had a disagreement with Falcon. *I should have just checked into a hotel until I found an apartment to rent,* Ree thought as she listened to her mother bitch. Ree searched online for an apartment, knowing that her move would have to be real soon because her mother wouldn't stop talking about what she would do to Falcon when she saw him. *This apartment in Overland would be great for me, but it doesn't have a washer and dryer hook-up and that's a must-have*, Ree thought. She excused herself from her mother's bitching to call Tower Haven Apartments, praying that the unit she saw online was available. Larissa, the woman who answered the phone, let Ree know the apartment hadn't been taken and offered to schedule a tour for Ree within the next week. "I would like to see the apartment today, like say in an hour, if possible," Ree said.

"Sure, that's not a problem. I'll be waiting in the leasing office, Ms. Street," Larissa said.

Ree thanked Larissa for allowing her to come on such short notice and rushed to take a shower while listening to her mother tell her personal business to one of their family members on the telephone. *And that's why I can't stay here,* Ree thought, shutting the bathroom door.

C' That's Why I Don't Fool with Women

My New Future Place to Live

When Ree walked into the leasing office, she was greeted by Larissa Slap. The ladies shook hands and engaged in small talk before going across the street to look at the apartment. Ree was trying not to get all excited about the restaurants and ladies' boutique in walking distance that she would explore if she moved into the neighborhood. Larissa unlocked the door and allowed Ree to enter the apartment first to give her a feel of what the place would be like as her new home. The apartment was fully furnished with hard wood floors and a balcony with a beautiful view of the city. "I love it," Ree said as she continued to walk through the two-bedroom apartment. *Checkmate,* Ree thought when she saw the washer and dryer that came with the apartment.

"We can go back to my office and fill out the paperwork," Larissa said, hoping that she had a new tenant moving in soon to get a bonus for meeting her quota for the month. Since the computer system was down, Larissa asked Ree to give her a call back in the morning after 10 a.m. after all the paperwork was verified through the main office. When Ree left the leasing office, she went shopping for things for her new place. As Ree drove down Page Ave. crossing Lindberg, she thought about finding furniture that was like what was in the apartment, because she loved every damn thing about the place. As Ree headed to the furniture store, her ringing cell phone broke her concentration. She figured it was Falcon. "Yeah, what the hell do you want?" Ree said, ready for the verbal battle since Falcon got out of jail right away as she expected.

"Ah no, this ain't Falcon," the caller said.
"Ila wass up girl?" Ree asked as she drove in traffic.
"It seems like you're having man problems at home too, girlfriend," Ila said, feeling a little down in spirit.

Ree ignored Ila's comment about man problems. She wasn't into telling what went on in her marital life. She had learned many years ago that a woman can change their ways and use what you told them in confidence against you. "Wass up Ila?" Ree asked.

"I'm calling you for a couple of reasons since you called in today and I couldn't talk to you at work. Hampton and I got into it, and I told him I was with you all night long till Sunday morning, which is kind of true, but a boldface lie as well because I didn't mention the club," Ila said.

"You sound horrible. What time do you get off so that we can talk about your situation?" Ree asked, feeling like something just wasn't right with her friend.

"I don't get off till 7, and I just want to go home and go to sleep when I get off work," Ila said. *Shit, my side is hurting, and I don't feel like going back. All my patients are bedridden and the patient care tech working with me is a little white prissy petite person that looks like she can't lift her own damn finger to assist herself,* Ila thought. She really felt like Hampton broke her ribs after he raped her, but she was too afraid to go to the emergency room to get checked out because she was a registered nurse at the hospital.

C' That's Why I Don't Fool with Women

"Well if you change your mind give me a call so we can meet up," Ree suggested.

"Will do, let me get to my patients before I get written up for some bullshit," Ila said.

"I understand. Don't hesitate to call me if you need to talk," Ree said before hanging up.

Ree pulled up at the furniture store and saw a familiar face. It was Del'Feela, one of Ila's friends. *Damn, she looks totally different from the girl's night out at the club*, Ree thought. Knowing damn well the bitch felt some kind of way toward her, Ree took it upon herself to speak first and keep it moving. "Hey Del'Feela," Ree said and kept on walking toward the front door of the furniture store.

Del'Feela was surprised that Ree even acknowledged her because she said less than two words to her at the girl's night out Saturday night. "Hey Ree," Del'Feela said, but Ree had already gone in the store and didn't hear her. Del'Feela had hooked up with an organization that helps people with low income after telling them her home flooded. With a voucher from the organization, Del'Feela could spend up to a $1,000 in the clearance department. That made the value of the voucher stretch a long way. Ree watched from afar as the men loaded Del'Feela's truck with a head and foot board for a bed along with a box spring and mattress, two-night stands and two lamps. "Thank you so very much for your help guys," Del'Feela said as she shut the door to her boyfriend's truck before driving away without giving a tip.

Ree walked through the furniture store to see if anyone would assist her but all the brothers and sisters walked by her as though she was just window shopping and couldn't afford to buy one thing. *This is a shame that my own people are walking by and I want them to make the commission, but it looks like this little old white lady is going to get this money instead*, Ree thought.

Sherre Still

"Hello ma'am, may I help you with something today?" the little old white woman asked with such a pleasant smile.

"You sure can, ma'am" Ree replied. Ree pointed to the bedroom set she was standing next to and asked the woman to point here to the Italian rugs and the other decors for her apartment.

"Ma'am what is your name? You have such great taste in such exquisite things," the little old white lady said.

"My name is Ree, ma'am, and exquisite things are what I'm used to," she replied. By the time Ree left the furniture store, she had bought everything almost identical to what was in the apartment she was going to rent. The little old white sales lady had gone in the back to get Ree a glass of champagne as she totaled her bill of sale with a smile and saw the credit card approved for the total of $6,000. Ree left the furniture store with a free comforter set for her bed that the little old white lady gave her that she literally paid for. The black salespeople had displeased looks on their faces as though she should have begged them to wait on her to make a sale. Just as Ree felt like her mission was accomplished, Falcon called. *I'm sending his ass to voicemail, because he's not privileged to talk to me until we sit down with our lawyers*, Ree thought as she drove to her mother's home.

When Ree arrived at her mother's house, nobody was home. Ree decided to order Chinese food and got enough for her mom to avoid any complaining from her. Ree called in the order and went to pick up the food. By the time Ree got back with food, her mother was sitting at the kitchen table eating a burnt bologna sandwich. Ree knew what her mother was going to say as soon as she smelled the Chinese food. "So you didn't think about buying me anything to eat, huh?" Violet asked.

C' That's Why I Don't Fool with Women

"Momma, I know you like a book. Here's your chicken egg foo young along with the crab rolls that you love from Chop Suey. Can I get a thank you please?" Ree asked with a smile.

"Thank you," she said. "I went to pay your old man Falcon a visit since he ran you out of your home. That old ma'tha' fucka don't want what I have to give him, understand?" Violet said as she stirred up her food. Ree suddenly got sick to her stomach with the thought of her mother acting a fool out in the suburban neighborhood she and Falcon lived in.

"Momma, he didn't put me out. I left on my own free will because we had a disagreement. What did you do momma?" Ree calmly asked, hoping it wasn't too bad.

"Well, let's just say because Falcon was acting like a bitch and wouldn't coming outside to talk to me like an adult I busted all of the windows out of his car. I had to let Falcon know this is what women around his age, the ones he should be dating, would do," Violet said as she pulled out her cellphone to show her daughter what she had done.

Ree couldn't believe her eyes. The word BITCH was spray painted on both sides of Falcon's car. Knowing that she didn't encourage her mother to vandalize Falcon's car, Ree knew she would have to talk to her husband sooner than she planned. Violet listened to Ree voice her opinion and let it go in one ear and totally out the other.

"I'll also be moving at the end of the week. If not then, then by next Monday for sure," Ree said before going into her old bedroom to sit on the twin bed she used to sleep in as a teenager. Violet wasn't happy about Ree moving out.

"Ree, you don't have to move anywhere. Home is right here. You know that," Violet said as she finished eating her food. Feeling a bit tired, Ree pushed her twin bed and her sister's old twin bed together to make it a full-size bed and laid down to tune her mother's voice out and take a nap.

C' That's Why I Don't Fool with Women

7 p.m.

Ree's ringing cell phone woke her up. It was Falcon. "Can we please talk?" he asked, truly realizing his mistake and glad that his wife answered his call.

"Falcon, I want a divorce. We don't need to talk about anything anymore. You treat me like I'm your child, and I'm your wife. Who on God's green earth watches their wife coming and going from the damn security camera? You do. I've done nothing wrong against our marriage whatsoever for you to be acting the way that you do, and it's totally destroyed my feelings for you Fal," Ree said in tears because she still loved her husband.

"So, you are saying that you don't love me anymore?" Falcon asked, trying to prepare himself for what was about to happen.

"Yes, I love you Fal. I'm just not in love with you anymore. There's a difference," Ree said, trying her best not to let her husband hear her cry.

Falcon felt the pain he put upon his wife right then and there as he heard her crying. He was determined to try and make things right with Ree's mother first before approaching his wife, because he knew his mother-in-law would pay him another visit. "Falcon I got to get off of the phone. I'm tired and worn out. I need some rest," Ree said.

"Ok baby get some rest, but please promise me this. Can we please have a conversation later?" Falcon asked.

"I'll think about it," Ree said, not wanting to deliver more bad news such as she found an apartment. Falcon only hoped and prayed that there was a way to keep Ree as his wife.

Ila had a change of heart and called Ree because she was in excruciating pain by the time she got off from work and needed someone to take her to another hospital other than the one she worked at to get some medical attention. Ree didn't answer the first time. Ila called once more while sitting in her car in the parking lot, praying her friend would answer.

"Hello," Ree answered.

"Thank God you answered, Ree. Can you please take me to the hospital? I feel like shit," Ila said about to cry.

Confused, Ree looked over at the clock. It was 7:38 p.m. "Where are you?" Ree asked while putting on her tennis shoes.

"I'm in the employee parking lot sitting in my car," Ila said now crying.

"I'm on my way," Ree said. She hurried up to help her friend in need. Driving as fast as she could to make it to Ila's location, Ree hoped things weren't as bad as they sounded over the phone. When Ree parked beside

C' That's Why I Don't Fool with Women

Ila's car, she couldn't believe her eyes. Ila had cried so much that her make-up had come off of her face, showing her black eye. "What in the hell happened to you? I need to call the police, Ila," Ree said, thinking that her friend had been robbed or something.

"No, don't call the police. Just take me to the hospital please. I think my ribs are broken," Ila said still crying in pain.

"C'mon and get in my car. Your gas hand is on E," Ree said, assisting Ila as she got out of the car.

Ree drove on Highway 40 going west to go to the hospital off Ballas Road. When they got to the emergency room, the staff rushed Ila to the X-ray department, so Ree went to the chapel to pray for Ila's well-being. "Lord, what is wrong with these men nowadays? I think it's something that's in the water that they're drinking to make them act the way that they do. Please God don't let Ila's ribs be broken and mend her heart because her husband Hampton has truly shattered it. In Jesus name, amen," Ree prayed. Ree left the chapel and went back to the emergency room. Ree sat with Ila for about four hours. The right side of her ribs were fractured, and she was going to be admitted in the hospital. Ree left once Hampton came walking through the door of the emergency room. *Ain't this about a bitch? This asshole has fractured Ila's ribs and given her two black eyes and she texted this fucka to sit at her bedside*, Ree thought driving back to her mother's house mad as hell

Sherre Still

Good News

Ree couldn't wait to call the leasing office Tuesday morning to find out what time she could pay her security deposit and first month rent to receive her apartment key. At 10:40 a.m. Ree called after getting dressed and eating a full breakfast that her mother cooked.

"Tower Haven Apartments, this is Larissa. May I help you?" Larissa asked in a pleasant voice.

"Good morning, Larissa, this is Ree Street calling,"

"Oh, good morning Ms. Street. I have good news. You were approved for the apartment. What day and time would you like to do business this week?" she asked.

"I would like to do business today by giving you a cashier's check and receiving the key please around say 2:00,"

"That's an excellent time for me right after my lunch hour. See you then Ms. Street,".

Ree knew she would be approved, because she had excellent credit and didn't have any out-standing bills. Thinking ahead, Ree called the furniture store to arrange for the delivery to be Wednesday. Violet insisted on seeing

C' That's Why I Don't Fool with Women

Ree's new apartment because she just didn't believe her baby girl was separating from the old buzzard she was married to. Violet sat in the passenger seat of Ree's car not saying a word to rub her daughter the wrong way and make her bust a U-turn and take her right back home.

"Momma there's my apartment building over there," Ree said, pointing at the building to her left.

"The location is really nice, so that's one good thing," Violet said as she got out of the car.

Ree walked into the leasing office and introduced her mother to Larissa then asked her mother to sit in the waiting area while she signed the lease. Violet tried not to show she was upset that Ree asked her to wait in the waiting area. She wanted to find out how much her daughter's rent was going to be. Ree signed the lease and reached for the apartment key, praying that her new journey in life without Falcon would be a good one.

"C'mon momma so that you can see my new place," Ree said.

Violet followed her daughter as they crossed the street and headed to the apartment building. To the third floor they went with Ree putting her key in the door. Ree ushered her mother to walk in the apartment first so the she could inspect the place and ooh and ahh at the furniture and decor. To Ree's surprise, Violet had no complaints about the apartment. She was really impressed with her daughter's new living quarters. There is nothing more pleasing as a parent than to raise children to be adults that respect themselves and are able to take care of themselves. Violet walked over to her daughter and gave her a motherly hug and a word of advice. "Ree, I'm here for you and will stand by whatever decision that you make dealing with your marriage to Falcon. But, I am telling you if you go back to a man that ever puts his hand on you once he will do it again. I know Falcon heard me along with the neighbors. I told him that if I find out or you tell me that he's physically harmed you, I'm going to kill that old ma'tha' fucka and no one is going to be able to give him stiches when I'm through with him because he's going to be sliced like lunch meat."

Sherre Still

I Know She's Upset with Me but He's My Husband

Let me call her. I know she's upset with me, because she hasn't called or come to visit me, Ila thought as she applied her make-up. Ila had been in the hospital for a week and had been approved for a month of sick leave from work to get herself together physically and mentally. The phone rang as Ila got together in her mind what she was going to say to Ree.

Looking at Ila's name come across the screen on her cellphone, Ree debated about accepting the call, because Ila told her that she and Hampton were over.

"Hello," Ree said, trying not to sound upset.

"Don't sound so happy to hear from your friend, why don't you," Ila said, trying to make light of the conversation knowing it would get heavy if the subject was about Hampton.

"I'm happy to know you're alive since you're still allowing the woman beater to come around you," Ree said sarcastically.

"Listen Ree, I wanted to say thank you for being there for me when I really needed you. Hampton says that he's going to get counselling and that things are going to get better,".

C' That's Why I Don't Fool with Women

I shouldn't have answered the telephone to listen to this bullshit, Ree thought. Ila wanted her friend to forgive Hampton as she did. "Ila, can we talk another time because I have to work tomorrow and need my rest,".

"Ok, I just wanted to call you and say thank you whether you think I appreciate you or not. Maybe in a few months we can have couple's night out with our men,".

Shid, I ain't sitting at a dinner table and breaking bread with no woman beater, Ree thought. Speaking without thinking first, Ree shared her personal business when she normally wouldn't do so. Ila couldn't believe her ears when she heard that Ree was going to divorce Dr. Falcon Street. "Is this decision set in stone? It seems like he takes good care of you emotionally and financially,".

"I'm so set in stone with my decision that I've moved out of my home and into an apartment on the southside, and I'm not looking back. You're forgetting that I'm a nurse just like you and can take care of my damn self. Let me be your motivation to take a leap of faith and leave that asshole. I'm telling you, if I had been you and Hampton had done that to me I would be in jail for killing his black ass. I would love to see him in a man-to-man fight, the bitch," Ree said, thinking that she sounded just like her mother.

"Ree, I have to go. The nurse is here with the discharge papers that I need to sign," Ila said. That was a lie. Hampton had just walked in.

Sherre Still

Now Everyone Is Going to Know What Goes on In My House for Sure

It had been a week since Ila had been discharged from the hospital and Hampton was back to his same ol self, kicking ass and not caring what his wife's name was. *Ree is right. I need to leave before this man kills me*, Ila thought as she put an ice pack to her swollen right eye. When the doorbell rang, Ila rushed to put her shades on to tell the uninvited guest that she was just getting ready to go shopping for a Christmas tree.

"Damn, it's Zantaneek's nosey ass! Shit! Today is Thursday, and we always take our three-mile walk on Thursdays and I forgot to cancel," Ila whispered to herself standing behind the front door.

"I know you're in there, Ila. I can see you through the glass. Open the door. I have to urinate," Zantaneek said, constantly ringing the doorbell.

Reluctantly opening the door, Ila stood aside and let Zantaneek come in the house. Zantaneek went to use the bathroom and then returned to the living room where Ila was sitting in the chair holding her head down low. Doing jumping jacks, Zantaneek was proving to Ila that she was more than ready to

C' That's Why I Don't Fool with Women

burn some calories. Noticing that Ila wasn't moving, Zantaneek sensed something was wrong.

"Ila, why do you have on sunglasses in your house?" Zantaneek asked.

Ila just didn't have it in her to tell another friend the same story from a different day of the week that her husband kicked her ass for no reason. Zantaneek eased the sunglasses from Ila's face, seeing the unimaginable. As Ree reacted, Zantaneek felt and said the same thing. "Who in the hell did this to you, Ila? Does Hampton know about this?" Zantaneek asked, embracing her.

"Hampton did this to me, Zantaneek. He said that he wouldn't put his hands on me anymore, but he does it over and over again. I don't know what to do,".

"I say leave his ass, Ila. Have you seen your face in the mirror? I'm calling the damn police. Being a lawyer and a woman, you know I can't stand for this,".

Zantaneek convinced Ila to pack an overnight bag and go home with her before Hampton returned home. Ila knew Hampton would be home soon and if he saw her leaving with a friend he would definitely stop her from going anywhere. Feeling just a little stress relieved from her body, Ila was glad Zantaneek came to the house when she did, because there was no telling what the rest of the day was going to bring. "I haven't slept a full eight hours since I've been home from the hospital," Ila said. *When were you in the hospital? You never once called to inform me*, Zantaneek thought.

Ila called Ree once she got in the car and Zantaneek immediately got jealous but tried not to show it. When Zantaneek pulled up in her driveway, she asked Ila to wait until she walked around to the passenger side to help her out of the car and into the house, seeing that her friend was moving slow. After Zantaneek fixed Ila a bowl of soup with crackers and suggested that she take a bath to relax her mind, Ila felt comfortable but not able to sleep like she wanted to.

"Take one of my sedatives. Go in the guest bedroom and get yourself some rest, Ila. And please think hard about pressing charges against Hampton, because he's a stupid person to misuse and abuse you like this. I can see he's breaking your sprit to not fight against him. This isn't what people do that claim that they love someone," Zantaneek said.

Sherre Still

"I'm going to take your advice and go get me some rest," Ila said, walking slowly back upstairs.

Making sure Ila was upstairs in the guest bedroom, Zantaneek walked over to the wall to press the intercom button to hear Ila talking on her cellphone. She was talking to Hampton. *Ila has really lost her damn mind. I have rescued her like a stray dog and this crazy bitch has called this fool that's kicking her ass for fun as though she's a punching bag. Ila better not tell him to come over here because I'm going to put a bullet in his ass,* Zantaneek thought.

Tired of eavesdropping on Ila's conversation with Hampton, Zantaneek went to make a few calls of her own. She got Sharia and Del'Feela on the phone to gossip. "Now that I have my girlfriends on the phone, I got to let y'all know what's going on. I have nurse Ila in my house after I have come to her damn rescue from that good-for-nothing husband of hers," Zantaneek said. She was pissed off because she couldn't believe that Ila was talking to Hampton on the telephone like he never laid a hand on her.

"What you say Zantaneek? I know I must didn't hear you correctly," Del'Feela said as she tried to quiet her male friend down so his voice wouldn't be overheard.

"You got to be kidding me," Sharia said in disbelief.

All of them thought Ila had it going on because everything seemed to be so perfect from the outside looking into her material world. They were shocked to learn that Ila didn't have a happy home. Zantaneek also shared that Ila was in the hospital the week before with fractured ribs thanks to Hampton and that she called Ree to her aide and not any one of them. Now that was another subject to talk about.

"Why in the hell did she call Ree? How long have Ila and that hoe been friends anyway?" Del'Feela asked with an attitude. Del'Feela couldn't stand the sight of Ree or even the mention of her name. It pissed Del'Feela off even more because she knew other people who knew Ree and confirmed that the bitch really had it going on. Ree was a registered nurse and an entrepreneur. She was an author, property owner and more.

Del'Feela's male company pushed her by the head so hard that she fell back and hit her head on the headboard. "You on the phone taking shit with your friends when you should be taking care of your man," he said, putting his clothes back on to leave.

C' That's Why I Don't Fool with Women

Del'Feela was trying to whisper to tell him she was going to be off the phone in a minute, but she was too late because he was dressed and walking out of the bedroom door. *Got damn, I shouldn't have answered the telephone. Now I got to call my other boo for some money, so the fucking electric don't get turned off,* Del'Feela thought as she listened to Zantaneek run her mouth.

"I think Ila been friends with her since freshmen year in college," Zantaneek said while trying to tell her daughter that company was in the house. After talking for about another hour, the ladies got off the telephone.

Sherre Still

Men

Being under pressure from not being on top of his game in running the mechanic business that he inherited, Hampton dreaded seeing his mother Owna, who handed him the silver spoon to successes in life. He just had to run the business right, pay his taxes, buy insurance and not spend every dime the company made, pretending he had it all under control. Owna had been calling Hampton for weeks and leaving many messages for him to call her ASAP. *If I haven't called you after you left me 10,000 messages, why are you still calling me?* Hampton thought as he hit the steering wheel. He was behind on the business taxes and not sure if he was going to make payroll for the few employees who wouldn't just walk away to look for other employment. "Let me stop by the ATM so I can get a few more dollars since I wasted what I had on some fast food," Hampton said as he pulled up at the bank.

Hampton had Ila's bank card and could withdraw money whenever he wanted. Thinking large figures because Ila was the bread winner in his household, Hampton decided to withdraw $700 and rubbed his hands together as he waited for the cash. Hampton couldn't wait to go to the corner store and

C' That's Why I Don't Fool with Women

buy a case of beer and a pint of any type of cheap liquor to drink. "What the fuck?" Hampton shouted as "insufficient funds" flashed on the screen.

Hampton forgot that he wrote a check from Ila's account to pay an employee $950, overdrawing Ila's account. Driving away from the bank mad as hell, Hampton drove to the liquor store in his neighborhood to get two cans of beer with the quarters that he had in the astray for a broke day like the one he was having. Smacking his lips together and enjoying the ice-cold beer going down his throat, Hampton was satisfied for the moment now that he had a good buzz going on from smoking the rest of his marijuana as he drove home.

Ila had returned home to her husband after he begged and pleaded and claimed that he didn't know what he would do without her. Ila was sound asleep when Hampton came in the house screaming her name. *Why did he have to come home so early?* Ila thought as she looked over at the clock. It was 10:22 p.m.

"Ila!" Hampton screamed to make her get her ass up out of bed and cook him dinner since he had the munchies. Ila was ahead of the game and had a plate of food already in the microwave ready for her husband just in case he came home demanding something to eat right away. Dragging her feet and half-sleep from working 16 hours, Ila was worn the hell out when she stood before Hampton with one eye open and the other eye shut.

"Here Hampton, I'm going back to sleep," Ila said, heading back to the bedroom after placing the hot plate of food before her husband.

"Fuck naw! You ain't heading nowhere but to the damn freezer to get the ground beef to make me a fresh cooked hamburger and some homemade French fries since I can see we have a bag of potatoes on the counter over there," Hampton said.

Ila couldn't believe that Hampton was declining to eat the steak and baked potato that she had the cab driver pick up on the way taking her home from work. Hampton had totaled his car in an accident and now was pimp driving Ila's Corvette seven days a week. "Hampton, what have I done so wrong for you to keep treating me this way? I love you and try my best to comply with what you say, but you treat me like shit," Ila said now fully awake.

Hampton looked at Ila, wondering where she found the guts to let any words come out of her mouth after he just told her what to do right then. "Ila, shut the fuck up and do what I said now, because you ain't doing it. Don't put the ground beef in the microwave to thaw. I suggest you put it in some cold water and have it out all night till you cook the food how I want it prepared," he said.

Hampton got up from the kitchen table to feed their dog the dinner that Ila had brought him. When Hampton returned to the kitchen and saw Ila wasn't moving fast enough, he pushed her so hard that her head hit the side of the refrigerator, putting a dent in it. "I didn't do anything, Hampton," Ila said, crying her heart out.

"Hurry the fuck up before I keep your ass up till it's time for you to go to work bitch," Hampton said. He had such a sinister look on his face that Ila swore he would kill her.

C' That's Why I Don't Fool with Women

Facing Reality

Falcon told his children that he and Ree were having some problems, but he figured things would get better. "Daddy, things are going to be alright. You will be able to find another woman to take Ree's place," one of his daughters said.

Falcon had been served divorce papers at work with some of the nosy colleagues at the hospital asking what was going on. It killed Falcon to find out that Ree wasn't living with her mother and had rented an apartment. One of Falcon's nephews that worked at the post office tracked Ree by her change of address.

As a support system, Falcon's oldest daughter Lovette moved in with her father because she wanted to make sure Ree never returned to the estate she felt her mother should have been living in since she did birth three children by Falcon. "Can I ask you something daddy?" Lovette asked.

"Go ahead Lovette," Falcon said, knowing it was going to be a question about her mother.

"How come you didn't make mother your wife after she had three children by you and then supported you during medical school?" she asked.

"I've told you this same answer before, but I'll say it again. Your mother and I had grown apart and both decided to go our separate ways. We respect one another, and if she ever needs anything I will always help her out financially. So that's all I will say about that situation," he said.

Falcon didn't want to tell Lovette that she and her sister Pearlette weren't his biological daughters, but the baby girl Falkena did carry his DNA. Falkena was a splitting image of Falcon, and if she would call her daddy saying that she needed this or that she got it no matter what it was, because she was his baby girl, even though she was 30 years old and the same age as Ree.

Walking in the restaurant late as always, Falkena sat next to her daddy in the chair that he saved especially for her by discretely laying his leather jacket in it until she had arrived.

"Hey daddy, Lovette and Pearlette," Falkena said, happy that everyone was all together for lunch.

"Hey 'not so punctual,'" Pearlette teased.

Lovette got up to hug her baby sister, because she hadn't seen her in a while because of their work schedules. Pearlette caught Falkena up on the conversation about their father being lonely and needing to get back with their mother. "So, daddy what are you going to do? Leave the sweet young thing alone or beg her to come back to you because you're such an old man thinking you're not going to be able to get another young woman like myself," Falkena said, trying to make her father laugh.

Falcon kept his conversation with his daughters on a parent level because he never wanted to seem like their friend. "Ree and I are going to do what we need to do, and that's all you need to know," he said. With that said, they all ordered lunch and enjoyed each other's company, not wanting to upset their father any more than he already was.

C' That's Why I Don't Fool with Women

It's Strange How They Didn't Even like One Another and Now They Are the Best of Friends

Since the two women had a common denominator, which was Ila's safety, Zantaneek and Ree became civil with one another within weeks after not liking one another for years. Ila called Ree to let her know that she was finally ready to take that leap of faith after praying for strength to leave Hampton. After finding out her house was in foreclosure and they had just a few days to vacate the premises, Ila was emotionally drained and feeling down in the dumps for trusting Hampton to be the man of the house and handle all the business affairs. *Let me call Zantaneek since Ree isn't answering the phone,* Ila thought as she dialed Zantaneek's telephone number.

"Hello," Mantha answered.

"Hey Mantha, where's your momma at?" Ila asked.

"Hey Auntie Ila, momma is gone someplace with a lady by the name of Ms. Ree," Mantha said, trying to rush off the telephone so that she could get out of the house and go with her girlfriends.

"Oh ok. Tell your momma I called, and please don't forget," Ila said, pissed off as she hung up the telephone.

Sherre Still

Now how in the hell did these two become running buddies when they hated one another? Ila thought while she was trying to hurry up and pack a few things while texting a cousin to pick her up. She wanted to be long gone when Hampton got home from work. Ila had told Ree that Zantaneek was a lawyer that would fight to get her what she deserved in her divorce settlement, so she ended up using the friend-emy after the high recommendation from her friend.

"Girl things seem to be going well. Ila hasn't been asking anyone to take her to another hospital due to Hampton putting his hands on her," Zantaneek said, waiting patiently to hear if Ree was going to fill in the gaps with something she wasn't unaware of.

Ree didn't comment because she didn't want to get involved in the he said she said bullshit then physically be putting her hands on someone because of lies. Within the past month, Ree had hired Zantaneek to represent her as her lawyer because Saint Louis was small, and her husband knew quite a few people in the law business. She didn't think those people would respectfully look out for her best interest.

Zantaneek knocked on Ree's dressing room door so that she could give her opinion about a dress. "Ah no Zantaneek, that's not for you. Now you knocked on the door for my honest opinion, and I'm going to give it to you. Every style isn't for everybody, and that one ain't for you girlfriend," Ree said, shutting the door to put her clothes back on.

"Girl you know you can be a mess. I was thinking the dress was cute on me," Zantaneek said, looking in the full-length mirror to admire the dress.

Ree walked out of the dressing room so that she wouldn't have to give her opinion anymore since Zantaneek was trying to convince herself that the dress was really appealing on her. Since Zantaneek was taking so long to come out of the dressing room, Ree found a reason to spend some more money by going to the shoe department. "I'm going to the shoe department, Zantaneek. You can find me over there whenever you come out," Ree said, hearing Zantaneek ask her opinion about a different outfit she tried on. *This is my first- and last-time coming shopping with her ass because she takes all day to try on five pieces of clothing,* Ree thought as she tried on a pair of boots that she really didn't need.

"Well, well, well," Lovette said standing in front of Ree.

C' That's Why I Don't Fool with Women

This is going to be some shit. Last time I saw her there were a few choice words and some threats, Ree thought. Lovette was trying to move in and run the house Ree made a home. When Ree and Falcon got married, Ree laid down some rules the step-daughter didn't like. Ree let Falcon know that she wasn't going to be in competition with any of his family members when she was supposed to be number one in his life as his wife. Lovette came in on the argument her father and Ree were having and let Ree know that she was his daughter, and no one came before her, her sisters or her mother for that matter. Cussing and pointing fingers at each other went down and Falcon told Lovette to leave because she was upsetting his wife. Lovette never step foot in the house again until Falcon reached out to her to see how she was doing after Ree left him.

"Hey Ree, you're out shopping already and haven't received a settlement as of yet girlfriend. You better save as many coins as you can because living out here on your own isn't cheap," Pearlette said, giving her sister high five.

Ree had to stand on her two feet because she was prepared to fight Pearlette for calling her after Lovette left the house stating she was going to kick her ass whenever they crossed paths again. Falkena walked past her sisters to give Ree a hug because she loved the fact that her step-momma never once tried to stop her daddy from pampering her and they had a lot in common.

"Hey Falkena," Ree said, hugging her step-daughter. She was happy to see her to distract the scene.

Falkena let Ree know that her daddy missed the hell out of her and that she should go back home, because Lovette couldn't give the loving that her father really needed. Ree was laughing on the inside to see the two-bitch step-daughters frown up as they watched Falkena carry on a conversation with Ree as if they weren't even there.

"I know no other can give your father the love that I've given him, but I just had to leave him. Over time I'm sure one of the nurses at the hospital will be eager to sweep Falcon off his feet," Ree said, confirming they were getting a divorce.

When Ree was about to walk away, Lovette said something to make Ree stop in her tracks and respond. "Please Ree, give us all a break. You know damn well you didn't leave our father. He put you out for cheating on him," Lovette said, fishing for information that her daddy wasn't giving at all.

Sherre Still

This bitch just won't quit, Ree thought.

"Whatever you say bitch. I'll tell you this to your face, and I don't want you to forget it. When your daddy closes his eyes for the last time, just make sure you have your business in order so that you can take care of yourself. You too Pearlette because it's going to be hell for you two whores, I mean ladies, certainly. I have a job to take care of myself sweethearts, and what you two hate is you can see I'm shopping on my own dime, not begging your daddy for shit," Ree said as she kissed Falkena on the cheek and walked away since no one had many words to say after that.

Zantaneek was still in the dressing room after all that time Ree spent in the shoe department talking to Falkena and two people who were non-factors in her life. *Damn she's slow,* Ree thought, hearing Zantaneek calling for the sales lady to assist her. After spending another hour in the store, Ree and Zantaneek decided to get a bite to eat before heading home. *Let me call Mantha to find out if she wants me to bring her something to eat,* Zantaneek thought as she parked her Benz at the restaurant. Zantaneek waited patiently until her daughter answered the telephone.

"Hi mother," Mantha said with her friends laughing in the back ground.

"Mantha, where are you at?" Zantaneek asked out of concern because it sounded like she was at a wild party with the loud music playing in the background.

"Mother, I'm with friends at the bowling alley just having ordinary fun as a teenager. There's no drugs or sex going on nor alcohol around, ok?" Mantha said with an attitude.

"Mantha, don't get sassy with me, ok? I will come where you are and kick your want-to-be-grown ass, understand? Now, I'm going to start this conversation over with you and you're going to answer me without all of what you said before," Zantaneek said with an attitude.

"Woo," Mantha friends said. Mantha had her mother on speaker phone.

Mantha took her mother off speaker phone to have a decent conversation. "Mom, I'm out with my friends at the bowling alley by the house and will be home in about an hour," she said.

"Oh ok. Would you like for me to bring you something to eat or are you going to eat while you're out?" Zantaneek asked, trying to treat Mantha like a responsible teenager.

C' That's Why I Don't Fool with Women

"I'm going to eat while I'm out with my friends. Oh, Auntie Ila called for you, and I told her you were gone with Ms. Ree," Mantha said.

Zantaneek figured Ila was going to be pissed about them hanging out after business hours. Ree and Zantaneek walked into the Italian restaurant and were seated right away. Both women stopped when they saw Hampton being hand feed spaghetti by a young lady who looked to be young enough to be his daughter. On the J.O.B., Zantaneek pulled out her cellphone so that she could have proof to show Ila to give her motivation to leave that asshole.

"This nigga is so disrespectful," Ree said, about to confront Hampton.

Zantaneek grabbed her arm to stop her. "It's not your battle," she said. "I'm going to show these pictures to Ila and if she doesn't leave Hampton after this stunt then I'm going to put an end to our friendship," Zantaneek said, walking away after taking a few more pictures of the two all hugged up together.

I wouldn't end the friendship, but I certainly wouldn't be involved in her relationship anymore, Ree thought.

After eating dinner, Zantaneek was ready to take Ree to her car that was parked at her house, so she could go out for drinks with Del'Feela and Sharia if they were free to hang out. At first Ree wasn't up to being bothered with Del'Feela and Sharia because she wasn't willing to give them a chance to be in her inner circle. But then Ree had a change of heart to go hang out anyway after Zantaneek begged her to just have at least one drink. Zantaneek called Del'Feela and Sharia to let them know she was on her way to the club. She didn't tell them Ree was coming. *This is going to be interesting,* Ree thought as she walked side by side with Zantaneek. Del'Feela and Sharia had their backs to them. Zantaneek tapped them both on their shoulders. Their smiles immediately turned into frowns when they saw Ree standing beside their friend. *C that's why I really don't fool with women. They can be so fake and not even realize it*, Ree thought. With just a wave hi and smile to Sharia and Del'Feela, Ree told Zantaneek that she was going to see a friend she spotted in the club when walking in to avoid being bothered with the two she wasn't vibing with.

"Coop what's up?" Ree said, happy to see him.

"I'm good Ree. You still looking good from the last time I saw you. That's what I like about you. You're always together," Cooper said, handing Ree a drink.

"No, no Coop. I didn't see the bartender pour that drink, so you know I'm not going to accept it," Ree said. Cooper said that he understood. He drank that drink and ordered another one for Ree.

"I forgot your rule, but I didn't do you like that when I first met you and you had a drink sitting at the bar for me," Cooper said.

The bartender handed the drink he poured to Cooper and Cooper handed it to Ree. "Thank you very much. Cheers," Ree said, taking a seat beside Cooper.

Del'Feela, Sharia and Zantaneek just analyzed what was going on with Ree and the guy they remembered her dancing with at the other club when they went out for girls' night a while back.

"So Zantaneek, is your newfound friend still married or what? She is carrying on like she's a single lady with that dude I remember her dancing with from girls' night out at the other club," Del'Feela said out of jealousy. She had tried to get Cooper's attention when she first saw him and was rejected.

"Actually, Ree is getting a divorce, and I'm her lawyer," Zanataneek said as she got up from the table when a dude asked her to dance.

As soon as Zantaneek went to the dance floor, Del'Feela and Sharia began to talk. "So that's how this chick became friends with Zantaneek. Our girl is making money off the bitch," Sharia said, still looking over at Ree laughing and talking with the dude whose name they at least wanted to know.

C' That's Why I Don't Fool with Women

I Know I'm Going to Hear Some Shit

Ree took the elevator to the psychiatric floor where Ila worked as a registered charge nurse. When Ila saw Ree coming her way, she was going to act like she didn't even see her coming but she wanted to give her a piece of her mind, feeling betrayed by a friend. Writing notes at the nurse's station pretending as though she was busy, Ila stayed focused until she heard Ree calling her name.

"Hey, you," Ree said, ready for Ila to give her an earful because she knew that her friend was informed by Zantaneek's daughter that they were together without her being invited.

"Don't 'hey you' me, Ree. Let's go in the breakroom so everyone won't know my damn business," Ila said as she watched some of her co-workers looking dead at her as she spoke.

Ree followed Ila to the breakroom. She didn't mind talking to Ila because that's what friends are supposed to do. Both women sat down not smiling ready to have a heart-to-heart conversation.

"Ree Street what's up with you hanging out with my friends without me?" Ila asked, still looking mad as hell.

Sherre Still

"Ah Ila I do believe that in this country I can go and hang with anyone that I please," Ree said due to her friend coming at her in the wrong manner.

"Ree, I can remember almost a month ago that you couldn't stand Zantaneek and she didn't like your black ass either. When I called you both yesterday, my calls went straight to voicemail. Then I called Zantaneek's house and my niece tells me that you two are hanging out together after business hours without me," Ila said.

Now ain't this some shit right here, Ree thought.

"As I can remember Ila, it was you who suggested I give her a chance because Zantaneek isn't the bitch I thought she was. I didn't know there was a timeframe that I could communicate with Zantaneek but now that I am aware, cool," Ree said, about to leave the breakroom to go get a quick bite to eat because her lunch break was almost over. She was totally done with the conversation with Ila.

"If you want to be the first to know some good news, I'm leaving Hampton," Ila said, wanting to hear what Ree would say.

"About time, Ila; congratulations," Ree said before walking toward the door.

"That's what I called you for last night to tell you that I left Hampton for good this time. I'm staying in a hotel, so Hampton won't upset my parents trying to find me," Ila said.

Ree walked out of the breakroom and didn't bother to respond because she was pissed off about Ila trying to control her moves with people she had connected her with thinking that she might backstab her. While riding the elevator, Ree glanced at her cellphone seeing that she had a text message from Cooper. "Hey, Ree I know you said you had to work last night, but I was wondering if you wanted to go out for dinner tonight. Call me," the text said.

Ree wondered if she should go out on an official date with Cooper because she was still legally married. "Hmm… I don't know about going on a date with Cooper because ol' boy might get some ass certainly, because I haven't had sex since before Falcon went out of town to the doctor's convention," Ree said to herself before getting off the elevator.

Ree spoke to a few people who worked in other parts of the hospital while she paid for a sandwich and a drink. Then she headed back to the medicine floor where she worked. Just as she finished getting her lunch, Ree's

C' That's Why I Don't Fool with Women

cellphone rang. It was Falcon. *I wonder what he wants,* Ree thought when she answered the phone.

"Hey Ree, how's everything going?" Falcon asked, really wanting to know how his wife was doing.

"I'm doing ok, Falcon. What are you calling me for? My mind is made up, and I don't want to send you any mixed messages by communicating with you when we are going through a divorce,".

"Ree, things really don't have to be this way. You're telling me that after 10 years of marriage you're really ready to throw in the towel and say to hell with our marriage?" he asked.

"Yes, because your aggression and being physical with me has escalated to another level. I have a friend who is getting her ass kicked, and she's convinced that things are going to get better because her spouse is saying that he's sorry and things are going to get better. I don't want to experience none of that in my life,".

"Ok Ree, I really want you to know that I love you and that will never change sweetheart. I remember you being in nursing school and not knowing if you really wanted to finish the program until you found out I was a doctor. You wanted to see me every day," Falcon joked, trying to at least get a laugh out of his wife before ending their conversation.

Ree laughed while standing at the medication pixes getting some meds for a patient she was about to tend to. "No Fal, I wasn't undecided with my career, honey. I was trying to decide if I was going to transfer to another nursing program elsewhere due to you stalking me," she joked back.

Falcon now had hope that just maybe he had a chance to save his marriage with his wife joking right back at him, which he thought was a good sign. "Well Ree I'm not going to hold you knowing that you're at work, but I wanted you to know that I still love you. Have a good day," he said. "You do the same Fal,".

Sherre Still

It's Just a Date

Ree put Cooper off for a week before accepting his invitation out to dinner, because she was busy working and finishing unpacking her things in her new apartment. "So Ree I'm glad you accepted my invitation for dinner because I don't know if I was going to attempt asking you out again. It's only so many times a brotha like me can be rejected," Cooper said.

Ree just gave Cooper the "boy please give me a break" look while sipping her wine. "So, what are you going to order?" Ree asked while analyzing the menu to figure out what she wanted to eat.

"I'm going to order fried chicken with mashed potatoes, gravy and another beer," he said.

"I'm going to have the shrimp risotto and salad,".

"Sounds good! Get whatever you want,".

The waitress took their orders and quickly came back with two glasses of water and then their food. Dinner was delicious and the conversation was great. Ree was really intrigued with Cooper. "So, can we have more drinks at your place or what?" Ree asked with a friendly smile.

"Let's get going," Cooper suggested. He tossed a $100 bill on the table and told the waitress to keep the change.

C' That's Why I Don't Fool with Women

Ree drove her car to meet Cooper on the date just in case he was a psycho. Making sure Ree was following him, Cooper looked in his rearview mirror thinking it just might be his lucky night. Ree was educated, didn't have any children and was willing to have at least one Cooper found out in conversation. Plus, she had a good job working as a registered nurse. *I got to make Ree my woman once she gets that divorce finalized because I'm tired of dating these women who can't even meet me half way financially,* Cooper thought. Cooper had been dating random women who were on government assistance not trying to do better and blue-collar women used to working minimum wage jobs and not trying to do better. Being a gentleman, Cooper unlocked the door to allow Ree to walk inside first as he turned the light on. Ree stepped aside as Cooper walked in the house, locking the door behind him.

"Welcome to my home, Ree. Make yourself comfortable while I get something to drink," Cooper said as he walked to the kitchen.

Ree sat on the couch and reached for the television remote to find something decent to watch. Cooper came back into the living room with a bottle of wine unopened, so she could see him do the honor of opening the bottle in front of her. "Oh, Cooper you are such a gentleman," Ree said, reaching for the chilled wine glass while Cooper opened the wine bottle.

"So Ree do you mind telling me how soon your divorce will be finalized?" he asked.

Ree was taken aback. *Damn, is Cooper in need of a woman or what?* she thought.

"It's hard to determine a timeframe Cooper because there are a few things we have to agree on before things are finalized. Now tell me something. What is it that you do for a living?" she asked.

"I'm in the real estate business. Most of my properties are in Louisiana because the investments were dirt cheap and the population has doubled after the flood. The interest on my return has tripled since then," he said.

"Do you have any children?" Ree asked, making it her last question for the night. The smell of Cooper's cologne was making her a little horny with the mixture of the wine she was drinking.

"No, I don't have any children but would like to at least help contribute to one child before I get old and grey as I told you during dinner," he said.

Sherre Still

"C'mon here," Ree demanded as she pulled Cooper toward her.

Cooper went in for the kiss that Ree was yearning for. *Thank goodness Cooper's breath doesn't stink*, Ree thought as she enjoyed the French kiss they shared. Cooper licked her neck and traveled down between her breasts, and Ree wasn't stopping him from going after what they both wanted. Pants and panties off, Ree had her legs gapped opened while watching him put a condom on. Cooper's body was chiseled like a sculpture of art. Entering inside, he humped immediately. There was no slow-motion winding and grinding foreplay from Cooper. Trying his best to knock Ree's vaginal walls out of the socket, Cooper was trying to put a hurting on her, but little did he know he wasn't doing a damn thing. *No, no, no,* Ree thought as Cooper kept humping and sweating like he was running track.

"Cooper, please get up off me. Something ain't working properly for you," she said, standing up looking around the floor to locate her clothes before going to the bathroom to freshen up.

Cooper got up from on top of Ree feeling disappointed that she wasn't enjoying the sex as he was. *I can't believe this nigga thought he was putting pressure on my pussy,* Ree thought as she washed her ass with a few paper towels. By the time Ree returned to the living room, Cooper was totally in the nude and massaging himself as the soft music played in the background. *I'm getting the fuck out of here,* Ree thought as she swiftly grabbed her clutch and car keys and headed toward the front door.

"Where are you going? I thought we had a connection going on here," Cooper said, getting up from the couch.

"Ah no Cooper we tried to connect but your dick wouldn't interact with my pussy right, boo," Ree said, walking out of the door.

How dare this whore try to belittle my groin like she was some kind of virgin, Cooper thought.

"Whatever bitch who fucks a dude on the first date trick ass bitch," he said, sticking his head halfway out of the front door.

Ree wanted Cooper's neighbors to hear what she had to say whether he heard her or not. "Any woman of my age who knows what she wants would fuck the first date if the dick was properly sized, so she could feel it, bitch! Shut the front door so your little wacker won't get hard, because I'm not coming back inside for you to get the pussy I was giving away," Ree yelled.

C' That's Why I Don't Fool with Women

Ree got in her car disappointed because she needed some sexual healing and Cooper wasn't the one to give it to her apparently. As Ree headed to her apartment, she took a detour and headed to the place she used to call home. She put her key in the lock, praying the locks hadn't been changed. She opened the door and tiptoed upstairs. She could hear Falcon talking on the telephone. *I wonder where Lovette's stupid ass is at in the house. What if Falcon has company in the bedroom and threatens to call the police on me because we're going through a divorce and I'm trespassing?* Ree thought as she tried her best to look around in their bedroom through the keyhole. Proceeding with what she wanted to do, Ree turned the knob to the bedroom door.

"Lovette, you're back home from your trip?" Falcon asked, thinking it was his daughter.

Ree walked inside the bedroom just staring at her husband who walked directly to her, picking her up into his masculine arms. Falcon kissed Ree's lips and thought of gently sucking her lower softer ones. "I'm glad you're home, Ree" he said as he laid her on the plush bed so that they could make love.

"Falcon, I am not home to stay. I want to fuck if you don't mind," Ree said, hoping her husband was down with her plan to only have sex and not make passionate love.

Falcon began undressing Ree as she did the same to him. To feel Ree's soft skin made Falcon's dick harder along with her touch. With some foreplay and different positions, Falcon was beating Ree's ass like a paddle to a ball with rhythm. Drops of sweat fell down Ree's back as Falcon continued pounding her like a beast. *Now this is what I'm talking about*, Ree thought as she laid still allowing her husband to do all the work. Changing positions, Ree rode on top of Falcon during round three, bouncing her ass cheeks on his lower half and watching his toes curl up. *My wife is trying to kill the old man,* Falcon thought as he admired her figure. For Falcon to be 65 years of age, he could put a lot of young men to shame and that was one of the reasons why Ree married the old man who knew the human body well. Filling Ree up to capacity while she laid on her stomach, Falcon whispered in her ear. "Think about us Ree and give us another try." What Falcon didn't know was Ree gave it a lot of thought and decided that she was still going through with the divorce. She liked the single life. Ree married Falcon one week after her 20th birthday when she hadn't experience life much on her own. Yes, Falcon treated her like the queen that she was but over time became possessive to the point she felt like she couldn't breathe. Now that Ree got a feel of the single life and financially could take care of herself, she thought it was better to stick with the decision she made.

C' That's Why I Don't Fool with Women

Monday Morning

"Good morning babe," Falcon said, smiling at his wife and giving her a gentle kiss on the lips.

"Good morning Fal. Don't you have to go to work today, because I know that I do at 3 p.m.," Ree said as she rubbed Falcon's chest with her finger tips.

"Actually, I'm on vacation from the hospital and then I'm putting in for my retirement, because I don't want to cross paths with you at work after the divorce," Falcon said.

Ree was now feeling bad that Falcon was going to retire from the hospital a year earlier than he originally planned. She knew that he was involved in a study that he was deeply committed to. "Fal, please don't retire because of me. Since the hospitals have merged, I'll put in for a transfer so that we won't cross paths," Ree said. She gently kissed his lips, assuring Falcon she was not going to interfere with his work.

"Can you kiss something else?" Falcon asked with a devilish look on his face.

It was about nothing but pleasing her old man. Ree gently grabbed her husband's manhood and kissed it. Then she began talking nasty to her husband as though she was a porn star. She smacked her lips and gently licked around the head of him as Falcon called out her name, moaning, "Ree, baby shit!" Ree licked the length of Falcon and then deep throated him. Falcon was trying his hardest not to bust a nut. Knowing that Falcon was satisfied, Ree decided to take another ride on her husband's manhood before taking a shower and going home.

Lovette came in the house calling her father's name. She saw her father's car in the garage but overlooked her stepmother's car. Falcon didn't hear a word because he was sucking his wife's tits trying to keep her from getting out of bed.

"DADDY WHAT ARE YOU DOING?" Lovette yelled when she walked into her father's bedroom.

Ree looked over her shoulder to say good morning to her stepdaughter who was older than her. Pissed off, Lovette slammed her father's bedroom door without saying another word.

C' That's Why I Don't Fool with Women

Woo Wee I Needed That

Ree woke up with a smile on her face just thinking about how her husband put it down on her sexually Saturday night and Sunday morning. *Damn that was some good dick,* Ree thought as she rushed to put on her nursing uniform to get to work in a hurry by 3:00.

Ila looked like she was back to her normal self. She was energetic and moving all over the place at work, keeping herself busy so that she would not focus on the turmoil she went through in the past with her husband. Hampton had made many attempts to get in touch with Ila, but she made it hard for him to get in touch with her until their court date. All of Ila's funds were depleted from her bank account, the house went into foreclosure and still Hampton wanted to whoop on her like she was a punching bag and rape her when she did not feel like having sex. She was finally done with her husband. "Arly, I'm going to lunch. Would you like anything from the cafeteria?" Ila asked before leaving the floor.

"No, I ate earlier but thank you very much for the offer," Arly said. Arly was the nursing supervisor.

Sherre Still

Let me see if Ree has time to get a bite to eat with me, Ila thought as she rode the elevator to the floor where her friend worked. Ree was at the nurse's station relieving the secretary while she was at lunch.

"Hey nurse Ila," Ree said, smiling from ear to ear.

"Uh uh bitch. Why are you so damn happy?" Ila whispered, asking when she already knew the reason because she truly knew her friend. Ree kept smiling to keep her friend guessing. The secretary came back from lunch and thanked Ree for relieving her and allowing her to eat during the 12-hour shift. Switching her hips from side to side, Ree walked in the breakroom to tell her co-workers to watch over her patients while she went to the cafeteria. As soon as the elevator doors closed, Ila and Ree's private conversation began. "Bitch, you were with Falcon, wasn't you?" Ila asked.

Ree smiled still. "Yes, I was," she admitted.

Ila just shook her head smiling. "I knew you two were going to get back together," she said.

"We are not getting back together. It's a long story, Ila; trust me," Ree said getting off the elevator as they walked to the cafeteria.

After Ila ordered her food and paid for everything, the ladies sat at a table that allowed them to have a little privacy. "Now begin talking Ree because I'm all ears to hear your story girlfriend," Ila said while eating her lunch.

"Over the weekend I went on a date with Cooper, that dude I met on girl's night," Ree said, getting pissed off just thinking about him.

"Who in the hell names an African American brother Cooper?" Ila asked with a frown.

"Cooper's parents, that's who, but anyway let me tell you the story because I need to hurry up and get back on the floor. Dinner was delicious. The conversation was good, which lead us back to Cooper's place. One thing led to another because I was horny, and he wanted the pussy I had to offer. This nigga was humping me like a dog in heat girl, and I was like I'm not feeling any pressure if you know what I mean. So, I took the liberty to stop homeboy from doing what he thought he was doing so I could wash my ass and get the hell out of there. When I came back out of the bathroom to grab my belongings to leave, Cooper was in his birthday suit stroking himself to music thinking we were going to continue where he left off. I was like ah I'm leaving and was out the door. When I got to my car, this asshole stuck his

C' That's Why I Don't Fool with Women

neck out the door like a turtle in a shell to tell me how he felt because his feelings were hurt that I was leaving," Ree said.

"Girl shut up! You are lying," Ila gasped.

"No, the fuck I ain't lying. I'm telling you nothing but the truth. Anyway, he was talking about what hoe fucks someone on the first date trying to insult me. So, I was like aw hell naw you can't shame me. Let me tell your neighbors what you're about shorty. I said someone my age fucks someone when they have an average size dick or an enormous dick, which he didn't have," Ree said.

"OMG Ree. I know a neighbor or two heard your crazy ass," Ila said.

"They sure did, but oh well. So, I was going to go home but I was still horny ya know? I drove to see if by chance Falcon was awake, so we could you know. He was up. Do you get it?" Ree asked jokingly.

"You're so damn nasty, Ree. Hurry and tell me so we both can get back to work or we are going to both be looking for employment,".

"Well, I used my key because he hadn't changed the locks yet. Falcon was surprised to see me standing there in the bedroom doorway. My husband swept me up off my feet, took me to the bed and undressed me as I did him. Passionate love we made when I intending to just fuck and get going home. The next morning my stepdaughter, dearest Lovette, came walking in the bedroom seeing us all wrapped up in each other's arms mad as hell,".

"No way, Ree! Your stepdaughter caught you in the nude?" Ila asked.

"Yes, way! Why are you saying it like that? I'm in great shape baby and his daughters hate it except Falkena. That's my girl. My nipple was in Falcon's mouth while I was on top riding him like a horse, so I looked over my shoulder to say good morning to Lovette. You are talking about a mad bitch,".

"Girl c'mon; let's get back to work," Ila said laughing

Ila wasn't convinced that Ree was truly going to divorce Falcon. There was something in her friend's eyes that was telling her that she was still in love with her husband. "I can't wait till 11:00 comes, and I give the nurse following me the report because once I get off I'm going home to sleep like a baby. This is my floor, Ila. I'll catch up with you later," Ree said before stepping off the elevator.

"Ok see ya," Ila said.

Sherre Still

What a hoe. I would have never told anybody that story, Ila thought. *Who in the world fucks a stranger without knowing anything about their health history and then fucks someone else within an hour with whom they are in a somewhat committed relationship putting their life in danger? I got to remind myself not to eat nor drink behind Ree's ass. Damn, I wish she hadn't told me that one. There are some things you just must take to the grave because others don't need to know your personal business.*

C' That's Why I Don't Fool with Women

Having Company at Home

Trying not to show any envy, Del'Feela kept smiling, being the pretender that she was, while sitting at Sharia's kitchen table watching the clock and watching her prepare dinner for the family. Sharia Bar had a beautiful family, home and decent husband. Wentzville allowed Sharia to come and go when she pleased and hired a babysitter when needed. Having a man that brought home a pay check and paid the bills first then kept whatever was left over was a blessing, and Sharia couldn't stop talking to her friends about what a good lover Wentzville was. "So what time you say Wentzville will be getting off, so I can be gone when he gets home?" Del'Feela asked, as though she wanted her friend to have alone time with her man.

"Wentzville got off at 4:00. He should be walking through the door any minute now," Sharia said, stirring food at the stove.

While Sharia's back was turned, Del'Feela quickly took off her bra so that she could get Wentzville's attention when he came walking through the door. She wanted him to see her nipples hard and at attention. Just when Sharia was getting ready to ask Del'Feela if she wanted to eat dinner with the family, in walked Wentzville with flowers in hand.

Sherre Still

"Hey baby, it smells good in here. What are you cooking?" Wentzville asked, smacking his wife's backside.

Damn, Wentzville brings home flowers too, Del'Feela thought as she posed sexy in the kitchen chair.

"I'm cooking Salisbury steak, mashed potatoes, green peas and tossed salad, your favorite. We have company so stop smacking my butt in front of company," Sharia said.

Wentzville turned around to see Del'Feela smiling at him jiggling her body to make her breasts move from side to side. *This whore won't stop coming for me. If I tell Sharia, it won't be a fight. Sharia would attempt to kill this so-called friend of hers,* Wentzville thought as he hugged his wife and kissed the back of her neck.

"Hey mister, didn't I say not in front of company," Sharia said, giggling and pushing Wentzville away.

Why is Sharia worried about what I see when she tells me every damn thing that goes on in their life? Del'Feela thought as she told the married couple she was going to get going. Del'Feela hated the fact that she had been after Wentzville since the day she was introduced to him by Sharia as her husband. When Sharia was pregnant all four times, Del'Feela offered to be Wentzville's fucktress with him declining every time.

"Why does that man love Sharia so much? It's always the dudes that are nice looking with an average looking woman by their side," Del'Feela said to herself as she drove to her boyfriend's house.

When Del'Feela arrived at Quail's house, she found a note on the door asking her to meet him at the pool hall. *Shit, I only have so much gas in my tank and this man wants me to drive to the other side of town,* Del'Feela thought getting back into her car to head to the pool hall. Quail was shooting pool and talking shit about his next come-up. He had applied for a part-time job with the other part-job that he had already in order to get full time hours out of them. Del'Feela met Quail online and thought she had struck gold with someone who seemed established, but they were both looking for someone to take care of them. Del'Feela put her dreams of dating a caregiver aside and fell in love with the part-time stripper. Del'Feela walked in the smoky pool hall like she owned the place, trying to get all the men's eyes on her as she jiggled her body parts while she walked toward Quail. Approaching her man

C' That's Why I Don't Fool with Women

from behind while he was about to shoot pool, Del'Feela placed her hands over his eyes. "Hey Q," she said.

Quail turned around happy to see his part-time woman until he noticed her attire. "Aye, what the hell are you doing walking in here dressed like that?" he asked, showing he had an attitude.

"Q what are you talking about? I'm fully clothed, so stop hating on your woman because all the men's eyes are on me," she said.

Quail grabbled Del'Feela by the arm and took her out of the pool hall so none of his friends could hear his conversation. It was a man code never to be jealous over a woman no matter what.

"Del'Feela you mean to tell me that you think I don't know your fucking character. Now let me tell you about yourself since you think I don't know a little bit about you, girl. Yo hoe ass walked up in the pool hall with no bra on and tities flopping all over the place with those tight ass pants on like you don't have a man. I won't be disrespected, especially in front of my homies. Do you understand?" Quail asked, pointing his finger at the side of her head.

The nerve of this online boyfriend to think it's hard to get another one. How dare he try to put me in my place as though I'm his woman for real, Del'Feela thought while thinking of the correct words to say to keep from getting her ass kicked.

"You are tripping Quail. I would never disrespect you in front of anyone. My feelings are hurt because you disrespected me by grabbing me like a piece of furniture when walking me out of the pool hall. I'm getting ready to leave since you apparently don't want to be bothered," she said.

Quail's friends came walking out of the pool hall to make sure their homie was ok. They knew of some of their friends being shot by their women. When Quail spotted his friends, he played the role as if he didn't give a care about Del'Feela, dismissing her. "Take your ass on home then. I told yo ass you're not going to disrespect me in front of my friends," Quail shouted so that he was heard.

Del'Feela got in her car without saying anything. She knew Quail was performing in front of his friends. *Broke ass bastard*, Del'feela thought as she drove past Quail who was giving his friends dap after putting a bitch in her place.

Sherre Still

Happy Hour 4 p.m.–7 p.m.

"Yes, I'm happy to be free of children and out with my girls," Sharia said, toasting Ila.

Shit, it seems to me you're without children all the time if you ask me, Zantaneek thought while clicking her drinking glass with the rest of the women.

"So Ree, what's going on with your divorce?" Del'Feela asked, trying to get the 411 while researching Dr. Falcon Street online on her cellphone. Zantaneek looked at Ree, signaling her not to talk about her case because the divorce battle wasn't over yet.

During the past five months, the ladies really became aquatinted and friendly toward one another and accepted Ree into their girlfriends' group. "I'm doing what's best for me. If you ever go through what I'm dealing with you will understand. Ok?" Ree said, clicking glasses with Ila, who knew what her friend meant. Ree wanted to say, "Bitch, it ain't none of your damn business what I'm doing in my marriage. When you get a husband, if ever in this life time, then holla at me."

C' That's Why I Don't Fool with Women

Since Del'Feela couldn't get any information from Ree, she went around the table to the next person to be nosey. "So Zan, are you trying to get your ex-hubby back?" Del'Feela asked as though she was joking but really wasn't.

Zantaneek just gave Del'Feela a look that signaled her to mind her own business. Ila excused herself, figuring that she was going to be questioned next, so she went to the restroom to avoid talking about her personal life. Pasadena walked in the restaurant directly to the table, hugging Del'Feela, who greeted her with open arms.

"Hey girl. Hi everybody," Pasadena said, speaking to the rest of the ladies.

All the women waved with a fake smile except Ree, who was genuinely friendly. Ree knew what it felt like to be the outsider introduced to the girlfriend's crowd. Pasadena sat her gigantic ass in the seat next to Del'Feela, talking as if the other women weren't there.

"Girl did you see that big ol ass that girl Pasadena has?" Ila whispered to Ree after returning to the table.

"I couldn't help but see the lady's rump shaker," Ree said jokingly.

Zantaneek leaned over in Ree's ear to make a comment about Pasadena's ass. "What did Zantaneek say because I know for a fact it was about the enormous ass?" Ila asked Ree laughing.

"Zantaneek said Pasadena's ass is going to be hard to clean when she gets old due to arthritis in her wrist," Ree said laughing.

Ila just shook her head, "Zantaneek is a damn fool, and she knows it," she whispered. Sharia came back to sit after calling home to make sure things were ok with the children.

"And who is this may I ask?" Sharia said, looking at Pasadena.

Who's this bitch asking 'who this is' like I'm some type of object? Pasadena thought as she stared at Sharia.

"Sharia, this is my friend Pasadena. Pasadena, this is my girl Sharia," Del'Feela said with a smile.

The women greeted each other and then turned their backs to one another to carry on conversations with their friends. Now Zantaneek took the role as the interrogator, asking Pasadena questions about Del'Feela.

"So, Pasadena how did you and Del'Feela meet because we haven't heard our friend ever mention your name," Zantaneek said politely.

Sherre Still

Damn, I just got here and haven't even ordered a fucking drink yet. These women are something else, Pasadena thought.

"We are friends from college, and we went to graduate school together. Ah what's your name again?" Pasadena asked sarcastically.

"My name is Zantaneek, hun. I'm a well-known lawyer in Saint Louis," she said with an attitude.

Pasadena was done dealing with Zantaneek the lawyer who wanted to be relevant to her and the other women. She decided to thank Del'Feela for the invite and head out. Del'Feela understood that her friend was leaving because the other women weren't friendly toward her, and she promised to call her later. As soon as Pasadena was out of the restaurant, all the women except Ree said, "So bitch you have a degree?" Del'Feela never told her friends she went to college.

"Yes, I do. And don't act so surprised ladies, damn. I'm not just a beautiful face with a bad ass body. I'm just tired of working so hard and not having shit to show for it. I'm on a manhunt looking for someone to take care of me and pay my bills. I worked all my life and put myself through school. I'm burned out from the corporate world," Del'Feela admitted.

Del'Feela had been working since she was 14 years old, using her sister's information to work part-time until she turned 16. That's when she started working full-time while going to school to help her mother pay the bills. Determined not to be like her mother on government assistance her whole life, Del'Feela promised herself that she would get her education because that was the key to success in life. After earning a bachelor's degree in business and going to graduate school, Del'Feela thought she was going to relocate with a well-paying job to pay her student loans and be happy. Life obstacles came Del'Feela's way when her mother became ill and she made the promise that she would never place her mother in a nursing home. Feeling obligated, Del'Feela stayed true to her word by taking care of her mother. None of her siblings pitched in. Del'Feela couldn't afford to put things in storage so she sold most of her belongings, practically giving her furniture away, and moved in with her mom. She felt depressed and unappreciated, feeling like she was the only one experiencing what she was going through. She started to hate on everyone who seemed successful.

C' That's Why I Don't Fool with Women

"Del'Feela, in the 21st-century you're not going to find a man to just take care of you and pay your damn bills. C'mon now. It's a two-way street in a relationship or you just take care of your damn self, especially when you don't have any children to take care of," Ree said, speaking her mind as if Del'Feela was her friend when she really wasn't.

"Let me tell you something 'Mrs. Have It All and Don't Know What to Do With It,' until you become a caregiver to a parent and have to take care of all of her bills, you can't give me your opinion," Del'Feela said, pissed off.

"Del'Feela, I'm gonna break it down to you. Nowadays most men want a young girl to date. They don't really want to be accountable for them by paying for a cheap dinner and possibly getting their hair and nails done. Women our age are considered too old to be dating and requiring a man to pay a car note and mortgage monthly. I suggest you consider using your education to get a better job and stop searching for a hand out," Ree said.

Del'Feela was getting ready to cuss Ree out for trying to put her in her place and humiliate her at the same damn time.

"Hold on Del'Feela, you and Ree don't need to go there with each other. Just chill out and let us all have a good time while we're out. But Del'Feela, I must say you could have shared with us that you had a college degree, so we could at least help you get a decent paying job. We all are connected to someone that can pull some strings," Ila said.

Del'Feela was now pissed with Ila, who she thought should be on her side completely, "Ila, shut the hell up please. None of you never once have come over to my house and asked if there was anything you all could do to help me take care of my mother. None of you bitches ever said, 'Hey, I can hook you up with a job' knowing that I work for a temp agency barely getting by. Speaking of something that everybody didn't know, Zantaneek did you share with Ila that you sent pictures of Hampton and his side chick in some restaurant to everybody's cellphone except hers?" Del'Feela asked, waiting for an answer.

"Excuse me waitress, can we get two more pitchers of margaritas please?" Sharia asked. The conversation was getting heated.

"Sure," the waitress said, walking away while listening to the argument between the ladies.

"What pictures?" Ila asked.

Del'Feela pulled out her cellphone to show the pictures to Ila since Zantaneek was lost for words. Ree just sipped her drink as the messy situation unfolded. When Ila saw the photos on Del'Feela's cellphone, she asked why she wasn't included in the group text.

"Ila, I simply didn't want to hurt your feelings," Zantaneek lied.

Del'Feela wasn't through starting trouble when she noticed that Ree was sitting too quiet, so she made her the focal point of the conversation next since she was lost for words.

"Oh, I left something important out also Ila. Your girlfriend Ree was there with Zantaneek at the restaurant when she took the pictures of your husband with the side chick," Del'Feela said, laughing her ass off on the inside when she saw Ree's head drop low.

Damn, Ila thought. Happy hour turned into an ugly scene. Ila's feelings were truly hurt, so she quietly got up from the table without paying her share of the tab, figuring her so-called friends could take care of it.

C' That's Why I Don't Fool with Women

When You Start Trouble It Sure Enough Comes Back Around To You

"Why me?" Del'Feela asked God. One of Del'Feela's siblings let their crackhead brother into their mom's house and he stole all the meat out of the freezer and her flat screen TV. *This doesn't make any sense that now I got to come up with food money until momma gets her food stamps or we won't have shit to eat*, Del'Feela thought as she looked inside of the empty freezer.

"Del'Feela!" her mother yelled.

Shit! What does she want now? Del'Feela thought as she walked to her mother's bedroom.

"What momma?" Del'Feela asked, trying not to let her mood show.

"I need you to give me $250 so that I can go to the casino with your sister," Manwella said, looking at her daughter to go in her purse and give her some money.

"Momma, it's the middle of the month. I've paid the bills, and now I'm trying to figure out how we are going to eat for the rest of the month or we are going to starve. You don't need to go to no damn casino, because you don't have any money," Del'Feela said, letting her mother know that she was pissed off and broke.

Manwella didn't want to hear that nonsense. She wanted some of the disability check that she thought was in the bank or it was going to be a problem. "You mean tell me that I don't have any damn money in the bank after you paid all of my bills? I ain't no fool," Manwella said, scooting up in the bed cussing and accusing Del'Feela of stealing.

Del'Feela had to walk away before she did something that she would regret. Del'Feela wanted to say 'fuck it' and move out to live her life by herself. *I don't have to go through this bullshit with momma every damn month. The utilities are $560, her medication is $970, her credit card bill was $176 this month, leaving momma with $192 to spend how she likes so how in the world am I able to give her $250 to give away to the damn casino? If momma wins, she is going to give the money right back to the machine thinking that she's going to win more money and not come home with shit. And that no-good ass sister of mine — that bitch is so conniving to plant in momma's head that I'm the one stealing from her. I know she put momma up to asking for that amount of money because Baptisia has maxed out her credit cards until she gets her disability check. Baptisia and momma live above their means,* Del'Feela thought, shedding a few tears and stressing herself out.

C' That's Why I Don't Fool with Women

I Didn't Do Anything and Now She's Mad at Me

Since their girls night out for happy hour, Ila hadn't talked to anyone from the group, feeling a bit betrayed. Ree took it upon herself to initiate calling her friend, knowing she was mad at her.

"1400 may I help you?" the secretary asked.

"Yes, may I speak to Ila Train?" Ree asked.

"Hold on please," the secretary said.

Ree decided not to call Ila's cellphone because she never returned her other calls. "Hello this is Ila Train," she said, thinking it was a family member calling about one of her patients.

"Hey Ila, why are you still upset with me?" Ree asked.

"Ree, you know damn well I'm pissed with you. How could you keep a secret from me?" Ila whispered, not wanting her co-workers to hear her using profanity on the job.

Ree was done trying to make amends and was going to speak her mind because she was just as pissed off as Ila was at this point. "Ila, now you called me to take you to the hospital when your husband kicked your ass not once but two or three times. I asked you to leave Hampton for your safety because I love you as a sister, and you cussed me out as though I had blackened your eye. Now when it comes down to your friend Zantaneek, I wasn't the one who spread the word about your personal business nor did I send any pictures of your husband with the side chick. Your so-called friend did that. So, if you want to be pissed off with me then fine," Ree said before slamming the telephone down, hoping she had bust Ila's eardrum. Ree's feelings were hurt because Ila was on some serious bullshit list trying to make her feel bad for her soon-to-be ex-husband's behavior.

By 6:15 p.m. Ila was hoping that Ree was in sight on the floor so that she could apologize because her friend was right. Ree was walking down the hallway talking with a co-worker when she saw Ila standing at the nurse's station asking for her. Pretending like she was busy, Ree stepped into one of her patient's rooms to do some charting before getting off from work. Ila saw Ree walk into the patient's room thinking that she was now mad and avoiding her. *Ree can be so stubborn at times,* Ila thought as she walked down to the patient's room. "Ree can you step out in the hallway please?" Ila asked.

Ree reluctantly stopped charting to log out of the computer to talk to her friend in private. Ila placed her hand on Ree's shoulder. "Ree, I'm sorry for being upset with you when I shouldn't have been. You're right about everything that you said. Do you accept my apology?" Ila asked.

"Girl bye! Get to your floor and make some money so that you can buy me lunch Friday when we're both off work," Ree said as she hugged Ila before going back to the patient's room to finish charting.

C' That's Why I Don't Fool with Women

Gossip

"Girl if you had been there to catch Ree and daddy having sex I know you would have kicked Ree's ass honey, because I was close to doing so but I was worn out from the flight back home," Lovette said.

"I still can't understand why you two hate Ree so much after all of this time. I must admit when they first got married I was leery of Ree's intentions with daddy, but over the years she's earned my trust. Ree makes daddy happy, and married couples break up and make-up all the damn time. No one's perfect. At daddy's age at least he isn't sick, and we're not stuck taking care of him and going out of our minds because we can't have lives of our own. Caring for the elderly can be something else. Ask our cousin Maxine who owns a private duty business here in Saint Louis. Maxine told me at the family reunion about her employee having sex in the client's house and getting caught on tape stealing valuables. I was like girl you must write a book, because if you don't I sure will. So, with that said, I congratulate their love. Don't hate on their separation, because they're getting back together," Falkena said, trying to get her older sisters to understand where she was coming from. Pearlette and Lovette looked at their little sister as though she was crazy.

"Lovette, you're right though. If I would have caught daddy in the act, I would have been fighting that bitch," Pearlette said, pounding her fist in her hand.

"Well y'all, I need to pick my bundle of joy up or the daycare will charge me for every 15 minutes I am late," Falkena said, getting up from the table with her to-go bag and leaving her sisters to take care of the tab.

"Falkena just feels the way she does about daddy's marriage because she likes older men herself and Ree is her age. They relate the most since they are both gold diggers," Lovette said, ordering another drink and paying the tab for lunch.

C' That's Why I Don't Fool with Women

The Boys Will Be Boys

The fellas all held up their drinking glasses. "To the fellas," they said. Bellow, Falcon, Wentzville, Hampton and five other friends were at the men's club having drinks and smoking cigars while they swapped stories. The secret wasn't out that Hampton was a woman beater. He knew he wouldn't be accepted by Bellow, who was a judge, and certainly not Falcon, who was a doctor that saw battered women almost every day.

"Judge Clifford, have the criminal cases become more normal nowadays?" Wentzville asked, looking serious while sipping his drink.

"No, I deal with crazy and sometimes deranged criminals," Bellow said smoking his cigar.

"And what about you Dr. Street; are the stories any crazier than what I see on the news?" Wentzville asked.

"Gentlemen, I would say that I've never seen so many battered women come through the emergency room who don't want to press charges on the men. Men who beat women are weak. Men need to walk away when a woman gets on their nerves or the pressure is on them to physically harm their woman," Falcon said, taking heed to his own advice.

Hampton's conscience began to get the best of him and he knocked over his drink listening to Falcon talk about men who beat on women. "You alright, man?" the guys asked.

"I'm good guys. Just lost my balance is all. The next round of drinks is on me," Hampton said, knowing damn well all he had was lent in his pants pockets.

"No, you're not buying drinks. I asked you all to come and hang with the big boy so I'm paying the tab," Bellow said while shooting pool. Falcon talked about prolonging the divorce if he could so maybe he could get his wife to come back home as Bellow suggested. Hampton sat back and listened to his friends, thinking that all of them had some kind a problem. None of them were perfect men.

Since Ree's visit to the house, Falcon called her everyday as he did when she was at home to say have a good day and that he loved her. Trying to get a little more quality time with Ree, Falcon asked her to court him again, but she declined the offer. Hampton, on the other hand, had made many attempts to get Ila to come back to him by sweet talking her over the telephone because she was granted a restraining order. Hampton was stalking her on the job, so she knew her friends were right; if she went back he may kill her next time. After being served with the restraining order, Hampton agreed to get counseling to get his wife back. Hampton's business was closed because there wasn't enough money for payroll, equipment orders and utilities. Wentzville was wondering if he was going to tell his wife about her so-called friend De'Feela being so forward toward him. Bellow was at peace and had no complaints about his family life. He continued to talk about being blessed that he was still able to work and was still in good health.

C' That's Why I Don't Fool with Women

I Have Some Free Time to Myself

After having a guys' night out and sharing his problems with his homeboys, Wentzville thought it would be nice to get off early from work so that Sharia could have some time for herself. When Wentzville came home early and gave Sharia a few $20 bills to get herself something nice, she didn't know what to do with herself. "Thank you for thinking of me. You're such a good husband to me. Wait until my girlfriends hear this," Sharia said running upstairs.

Quickly, Sharia took a shower and got dressed so that she could hurry out of the house before her baby saw her leave and cried after her. Since Zantaneek's law office was nearby, Sharia drove there first to find out if she had some free time to have lunch. When Sharia walked in Zantaneek's office, she was greeted by the friendly secretary who let Zantaneek know she was there.

"Hey Zantaneek," Sharia said walking into her friend's office and taking a seat.

Zantaneek held up her finger, letting Sharia know that she was on an important call. "Ms. Clifford, I'm tired of you giving me the run around saying you were just getting ready to call me when I'm calling you all of the damn time," the client said.

"Ma'am I just talked to you last week and told you that I was going to call you this week and today was the day when my secretary said you called me," Zantaneek lied.

Underworked and never overpaid, Zantaneek always got her money up front from all her clients. Five of Zantaneek's clients had paid the required amount to retain her but she put work on hold to go on a three-day cruise with her daughter. When Zantaneek returned to work, she couldn't find half of the important documents that the clients had given her to handle their lawsuits. Still trying to mind fuck the client on the telephone, Zantaneek lied and said these kinds of cases take time and promised to call the client next week.

"Wass up girl! I was in court all day. Then I get to my office to a client calling me wanting to rush me with what I do best," Zantaneek said, letting her friend know she was upset with the client.

Word travels fast in Saint Louis and word was Zantaneek could be a bitch of a lawyer to deal with because her clients basically worked their own damn cases and still end up paying her for it. Sharia had to let her friend know she knew the real deal.

"No Zantaneek I heard the conversation, and that lady had every right to be mad, because what I heard her say was every time you set an appointment to meet her you're the one who is late. And we ain't going to talk about you and returning your calls to people, especially in your line of business. My cousin who used you said you were a slacker when it came to keeping things professional, Zantaneek. **It's bad when you patronize your own people and they bullshit you around**. I'm only telling you the truth because you need to hear it sometimes. And my cousin said she would never use you again for representation," Sharia said.

"That's fine if your cousin doesn't use me for representation ever again, but that's not going to put me out of business. As you can see and hear, my telephone is ringing off the hook," Zantaneek said.

"You're lucky that you're my friend because if not I'd be kicking your ass right now," Sharia said.

"Yeah and I'll have your ass locked up and will press charges for assault, Sharia. You know I don't play. So how long have you been harboring your

C' That's Why I Don't Fool with Women

feelings since you're letting me know how you truly feel now?" Zantaneek asked calmly.

Sharia didn't want to waste any more of her kid-free time with Zantaneek's foolishness. "Bye Zantaneek, I'll talk to you later," Sharia said, leaving her friend's office before things got out of hand. *C that's why I don't fool with women too much. They can be full of emotions. Sharia thinks she knows every fucking thing and don't know shit but how to get pregnant,* Zantaneek thought while pouring herself a drink to calm her nerves since the client threatened to report her to the state if she didn't get any results about her case soon.

Sherre Still

Let Me Call Someone Who Will Understand

Sharia didn't expect to be dealing with drama when she surprised Zantaneek at the office, so she decided to call Ila to tell her what happened. "You know y'all bump heads a lot because you both are just alike," Ila said.

"Me and that bitch ain't shit alike. I don't take people's money for a living and have them ringing my phone off the hook looking for me. Keep it 100 and speak the truth, Ila," Sharia said.

"So, what did lawyer Zantaneek do this time? Please don't tell me you recommended another family member that threatened to kick her ass because she didn't do her job," Ila said.

"No, I told you before I would never recommend her because she can be on 1 not 100 when it comes down to handling business. Zantaneek has too many things going on at one time and can't focus. Karma is a bitch, and it's going to bite that bitch hard in the ass when her day finally comes. I went to see if she wanted to have lunch since I wasn't free when she wanted to go out yesterday," Sharia said.

Ila just laughed as Sharia told her all about Zantaneek's angry client and their friend falling down on the job. "Now I would have to agree with you on

C' That's Why I Don't Fool with Women

that one Sharia. A person can be pushed to a limit. You can make a person snap and find that person waiting outside for you," Ila said. "I would say it's greed that motivates Zantaneek. She's not married to the judge anymore and lives beyond her means to make it look like she has it all together and can afford all the material things. It's sad to say but I'm not using Zantaneek for my divorce either, because I don't want to mix my personal business with our friendship and possibly have to kick her ass for not doing right by me."

When Ila's doorbell rang, she put Sharia on hold to see who was outside only to find Sharia standing on her porch. She opened the door and hung up the phone. "Now do you want to go out for lunch, because I'm determined not to eat alone or go home right away," Sharia said. Ila agreed to have lunch with Sharia and invited her friend into her new apartment while she got dressed.

Sherre Still

What's to Come?

After Ree was caught in the act with Falcon, Pearlette worried that Ree and her dad would get back together. She took some of her younger sister's advice and decided to call her cousin Maxine with hopes she was available to talk a couple of minutes about her father's situation. Pearlette was proud of Maxine and the successful businesswoman she was. When Maxine saw her cousin's name on the phone, she was happy to hear from her but hoping she wasn't calling for a handout. "What's up cuz?" Maxine asked.

"Aw nothing much! I wanted to know if you have a few minutes to talk with me, because our family is going through some things that I think you can very well enlighten me on since we're around the same age," Pearlette said.

"Yeah, I always have time to talk to family when there's a problem, Pearlette. What's going on?" Maxine asked, relieved it wasn't about a personal loan. She leaned back in her office chair to get comfortable, knowing that Pearlette could be long-winded sometimes and keep a person on the telephone for hours. As Pearlette talked, Maxine texted her secretary to ask her to hold all calls for at least an hour because she was on a conference call.

C' That's Why I Don't Fool with Women

"Daddy is going through a divorce with that wife of his. Ree is trying to work her way back in the house by giving daddy some ass after daddy put her out. Daddy is getting up in age, and I'm concerned that we're going to need someone in the future to take care of him since we know for a fact that heffa ain't going to be around,".

Maxine was thinking that Pearlette really needed to worry about something else after hearing what she called about because her Uncle Falcon was in good health. "Pearlette, are you sure you're speaking of the right person when saying you have concerns about your father? I saw Uncle Falcon last night, and we had a few drinks. He appeared to be in great health for a 65-year-old man. My friend was asking me to hook her up, not knowing he was my uncle. Uncle Falcon told my girlfriend himself that he was a happily married man and wasn't on the market to date,"

"No daddy didn't girl,".

"Yes, he did. I suggest that you not interfere in your father's relationship because it will only stress you out. People break up and make up all the time. Live your life. Now if you have proof that that wife of his is mistreating him then give me a call, and I'll be on my way. Keep in touch. Private duty is calling for me to work and make that money to pay the bills,".

"Ok Maxine! I love you, girl and thank you,".

"I love you too," Maxine said after talking to Pearlette for an hour and a half.

Sherre Still

It's Been A While Since We Hung Out

Since having their differences in opinions, the ladies went from days to weeks of not seeing each other. They missed each other's friendship, so they decided to get together for drinks. Ila and Del'Feela rode together and arrived at the restaurant first, so they ordered drinks and appetizers. When Sharia arrived, she complained about them not having her drink waiting on her when she got there. Zantaneek came in the restaurant looking serious because she knew for a fact that Sharia told the others what went down in her office a month ago.

"Hey Zantaneek, why are you looking so upset?" Del'Feela asked, trying to play it off like she knew nothing about Sharia and her getting into it with each other.

"It's been a long day at work and I'm just happy to be off is all," Zantaneek said. Then she turned her attention to the waiter to order a drink.

"Did you hear the comment Zantaneek just made like she's been really working on the job?" Sharia asked underneath her breath. Ila signaled for Sharia to be quiet to avoid another argument. Ree came in the restaurant

C' That's Why I Don't Fool with Women

looking around the room until she located the ladies sitting at the table. "Del'Feela, play nice," Ila said.

"Um-hmm whatever you say," Del'Feela said, agreeing to be cordial. Thinking her ears were playing tricks on her after hearing Ila tell Del'Feela to play nice, Ree spoke to the ladies and took a seat with a smile on her face. Del'Feela was eyeing Ree from head to her toe looking at her outfit. *This bitch is doing too much now. Ree didn't have to dress up like she was going to a wedding reception. Damn,* Del'Feela thought as she analyzed the name brand handbag Ree was carrying and designer dress she was wearing. Ree sat looking pretty and saw Del'Feela's eyes still glued on her. *This bitch is a mess*, Ree thought as she saw Del'Feela still looking at her. Back in the day, Del'Feela used to date Ila's brother Rusky a.k.a. Rus. Wanting to be part of a family with some means, Del'Feela wanted Rusky to be her future husband but he didn't feel the same as she felt. After she kept asking for at least a promise ring or asking to move in, Rus and Del'Feela were done.

The waiter came back to the table to ask Ree if she wanted to order an appetizer, but Ree didn't because she planned to leave. "Ladies, I just wanted to stop through for a minute before going home. You all have a good evening," Ree said. She hugged Ila and left. *Good riddance*, Del'Feela thought.

"So ladies how do you all feel about taking a weekend getaway trip together?" Ila asked.

"Will your best friend Ree be invited on this getaway?" Del'Feela asked, winking at the other ladies while dipping a slice of bread into the olive oil.

"Del'Feela, there's no need to be such a hater. We are grown ass women so can we please act as such? It's not like you'll be surprised if I didn't mention Ree," Ila said now irritated with Del'Feela's attitude toward her good friend.

Ree drove home after leaving Ila and her friends, second guessing her loyalty in friendship. *Why would Ila have me around her friends if they dislike me as I know they do*, Ree thought.

Sherre Still

They Don't Even Know

Zantaneek called her girlfriend to talk about the other ones in her life. "Mantha would you press the start button on the dryer before you leave the house" Zantaneek asked, relaxing on her couch watching cable. Mantha turned the dryer on and hurried to get ready to head to her father's house. When she heard the horn, Mantha ran up the basement stairs to gather her overnight bag and backpack in the foyer as she walked out of the front door.

"Momma can you lock the door?" Mantha asked.

"No Mantha, I can't lock the front door. You have a key; use it. You're so ungrateful. I can't get a break without you asking me to do something when I'm the one who takes care of you," Zantaneek said, feeling her daughter could be so lazy at times.

Momma has some nerve to say I'm ungrateful. If I'm ungrateful, I wonder where the hell I get my ungratefulness from since the umbilical cord don't fall far from my mother's body, Mantha thought while locking the front door. Thanking the Lord that she had the house all to herself, Zantaneek called her friend Pasadena. She was anxious to find out how she and Del'Feela knew each other.

C' That's Why I Don't Fool with Women

"Your friends are something else, and you played the role as if you didn't know who the hell I was, looking at my ass like you haven't seen it up close and personal before," Pasadena said.

"Let's not talk about that right now. How in the world do you know Del'Feela?" Zantaneek asked.

Pasadena had been out of town for a few weeks and every time Zantaneek thought about calling her it was too late at night or too early in the morning to call. "I told you and the rest of the girl crew that Del'Feela and I became friends in college. To make ends meet, we worked as strippers. We basically had the same struggles in life," Pasadena said.

"Now see you didn't tell us Del'Feela was a stripper," Zantaneek said.

Pasadena had to laugh at her friend's comment, not knowing the relationship between she and Del'Feela. Last year, Pasadena needed a lawyer and hired Zantaneek. One thing led to another as time went by and the two women fell in love. "I know that's a part of the story that I left out purposely, because Del'Feela's personal business isn't everybody's business," Pasadena said.

Zantaneek closed her eyes as Pasadena spoke, wishing they were in bed lying beside one another. Lately, Zantaneek had been wanting to ask Pasadena to move in with her because it seemed like she was never going to find a loving relationship in a male figure ever in life again. Paying for an escort service was getting old, and Zantaneek was ready to come out of the closet.

"Pasadena did you hear what I said? Zantaneek asked.

"Yeah, I heard you" Pasadena lied.

Zantaneek asked Pasadena if she would like to spend the night since Mantha was away spending time with her father.

Sherre Still

So Disrespectful

    Mantha was sitting in the passenger seat of her father's car letting her fingers go to work typing away on her social media page. *I'm so sick and tired of momma criticizing me, talking about how ungrateful I am when I'm not home living with her busy ass most of the damn time,* Mantha thought still typing away. Bellow made it his business to take Mantha to all her ballet classes and four days out of the week she lived with him and his wife Emi. Mantha didn't have an issue with Emi because the lady treated her like a daughter should be treated. Emi talked to Mantha about life, taught her important morals and took her at her father's request to be put on birth control after telling Bellow she was having unprotected sex. Mantha got out of the car and waved to her father. "See you after class," Mantha said.

    Bellow let the window down on his Chevy Suburban. "Mantha, I won't be picking you up after your dancing class; Emi will," Bellow said smiling at his daughter before driving away. Mantha waved again before walking into the building and winking at the security guard. Mantha had had a crush on the security guard since she enrolled five years ago. The security guard Strerow

C' That's Why I Don't Fool with Women

wasn't thinking about any of Mantha's advances toward him, because he had children her age.

Sherre Still

Let's Talk About It

Ila called Del'Feela. Then she called Sharia, so they could have a three-way conversation. "Sharia, do you see what Mantha's butt has posted on social media?" Ila asked while talking on speaker phone and preparing to go out with family.

"Yes, I did. Mantha is out there bad. I would find her and kick her ass as soon as I read this," Sharia said shaking her head.

"Well, all I'm going to say is Mantha is ungrateful and Zantaneek is crazy for trying to buy her love at the cost for such disrespect," Del'Feela said while preparing some food for her mother who just returned home from a day at the casino.

"You're sholl right about that, Del'Feela," Ila said, walking out of her apartment to see Hampton's car sitting outside.

"Ila where are you getting ready to go? I can hear your keys jingling?" Sharia asked.

Ila was tussling with Hampton, who was trying to put his hand over her mouth to keep her from yelling. With fighting for what Ila thought was her life, she yelled "HELP! CALL THE POLICE! MY EX-HUSBAND IS

C' That's Why I Don't Fool with Women

TRYING TO KILL ME!" Both Del'Feela and Sharia hung up the telephone to call the police and then head over to Ila's apartment. Rushing out of the house and getting into her car after talking to the police, Ila was trying to find Ree's telephone number to tell her what was going on.

Mantha's body was sore all over from the stretching exercises in ballet class. "Hi Emi, how was your day at work?" Mantha asked as Emi handed her an organic shake she had bought for her.

Mantha and Emi always liked each other. Mantha liked Emi's support and willingness to spend quality time, which was something Zantaneek wouldn't do. Emi just liked the fact that Mantha didn't see her as a threat since she was the other woman in her father's life. "Work was work, Mantha. Hey, we need to talk about something," Emi said while driving her BMW on the highway.

"What is it?" Mantha asked while sipping her drink through the straw.

"I saw what you posted on social media and wasn't happy when I read it, Mantha," Emi said in such a way wanting her step-daughter to feel bad for what she had done.

Mantha knew exactly what her step-mother was talking about. "My mother made me mad. All she talks about and thinks about is herself," Mantha said, trying to justify her wrongdoing.

"It doesn't matter how mad your mother makes you sweetheart. You're never to disrespect your parents. I would like for you to delete the post and pray that your mother nor your father read anything," Emi said pulling up in the driveway. Mantha reluctantly deleted every negative thing she had posted about her mother.

Hampton was sitting in the backseat of the police car in handcuffs, angry at himself for totally losing the woman that had his back. During the divorce hearing, the judge had warned Hampton to stay away from Ila or he would make sure he served time in prison after reading over the hospital reports that Ila's lawyer had presented. Hampton's intent was to ask Ila if they could talk when she came outside, but when she tried to run away, he grabbed her and punched her in her ribs like she was a punching bag. Del'Feela, Sharia and Ree all mean mugged Hampton as he sat in the back seat of the police car. "You punk ass bitch! Why don't you fight someone of your same gender?" Ree yelled.

Sherre Still

"Yeah you weak ass punk! Fight a man like you be hitting on our friend, so he can kick your ass you fucka," Sharia shouted before the police car drove away.

Devastated, Zantaneek was sitting at her desk when she read the social media post. Her daughter said she wasn't a lawyer anyone would want to use for representation because she's a bitch, a horrible mother and not a good wife and that's why her father left her struggling to work seven days a week to rip her clients off. As Pasadena read the computer screen over Zantaneek's shoulder, she thought *damn her daughter really hates her.* To make her feel better, Pasadena gently hugged Zantaneek, assuring her that things were going to get better between her and her daughter. "How can you recover when a child you birthed shames you to the world? My career is how I support us and this is how she disrespects me?" Zantaneek asked, laying her head on Pasadena's chest.

"I suggest that you go to work and act as though you did not even read it. Something like this will kill you if you let it. You know how the saying goes; it's your family or a too close so-called friend that will bring you down or try to take advantage of you. If Mantha hates you so much, I suggest you allow her to go live with her father and let her see how it is to be with him and his wife," Pasadena suggested.

"No, I can't do that because I need that child support that Bellow pays faithfully to pay my mortgage," Zantaneek admitted.

Even though Pasadena was an independent woman, she relied on the extra cash that Zantaneek gave her every two weeks. Curiosity ran through Pasadena's mind. "Zantaneek, are you broke?" Pasadena asked as she pushed Zantaneek off of her.

"No, I'm not broke," Zantaneek said as she wiped away her tears.

Intuition was telling Pasadena that there was something Zantaneek wasn't telling her and that she would have to snoop and find out since her friend wasn't volunteering any information.

C' That's Why I Don't Fool with Women

Family Time

"Mantha, dinner is ready," Emi yelled.

"Ok, I'm coming," Mantha shouted while talking on her cellphone with a friend when she should have been doing her homework.

"I see you deleted the post from earlier. Why did you put something like that on social media for the world to see? Did your mother cuss you out or threaten to put you out the house?" Phoenix asked.

"No bitch, my mother didn't see anything. She's at work as always not even thinking about me. I'm at my father's house where I'd rather live until I graduate from high school. I posted it because at the time my mother was in her feelings and called me ungrateful, which pissed me the hell off," Mantha said, laughing and trying to make it seem like it wasn't a big deal.

"Well if my momma was yours and had read what you posted she would have kicked your ass. You didn't get so many likes from your stupid comment either as you thought you would. You need some help," Phoenix said in a serious tone.

Mantha's smile turned into a frown because the last thing she wanted was to not be liked by her 1,000 social media friends. Emi called for Mantha once more to come downstairs for dinner. "Well, I'm getting ready to get off the phone because it's time to eat dinner with the family," Mantha said.

Phoenix just hung up on her friend without saying goodbye. Mantha walked down the steps thinking of what her friend Phoenix just said, hoping her mother hadn't read what was posted and thinking it would be hell to pay if she did. With seeing the look on Mantha's face, Emi thought the worst. "Have you talked to your mother?" Emi asked as they walked to the dining room.

Mantha plopped down in the dining room chair and prayed, promising to never disrespect her mother again if God was on her side with this one. "No, I haven't talked to my mother yet. I just got off the phone with my friend Phoenix and she said that my social media friends said I need to get my butt kicked because of what I posted about my mother," Mantha said, scared and about to cry.

Emi was worried for her stepdaughter because there were certain things that could be blown out of proportion that would turn into a fight, killing etc. As the ladies sat down at the dinner table, Bellow walked into the room, admiring his wife and daughter's beauty. "My ladies are waiting on the man of the house to sit before you to eat?" Bellow asked joking around. Mantha and Emi didn't pay Bellow's comment any mind.

"Bellow, we have a problem. Mantha has posted something negative on social media about her mother that I asked her to delete. Some of Mantha's social media friends are now threatening her and you can imagine what can transpire from that," Emi said as she sipped wine from her glass.

"You say what?" Bellow asked upset.

Mantha felt so ashamed because she knew how her father felt about social media and her being disrespectful toward her mother. As she watched her father shake his head, Mantha knew it was going to be a long night of preaching before she would be excused from the dinner table. Bellow couldn't understand for the life of him why children would do the opposite of what adults told them to do most of the damn time.

C' That's Why I Don't Fool with Women

Chain Reaction from Your Past Actions

Being used to getting away with kicking his wife's ass, Hampton thought he was going to get a slap on the wrist with short term probation and counseling as he listened to the judge read his verdict. As Sigel, Hampton's public defender, sat next to his client, he hoped to win this case so that he could get a promotion and move on to better things. Sigel was overworked and underpaid and wasn't working in the best interest of his clients. "You will serve 15 to 22 years in Saint Orris Prison," the judge said.

Hampton cried like a newborn baby because he just couldn't believe that he wasn't going to be released to have his freedom. Once Ila and her family members heard the verdict, they left the courtroom pleased. *It's something how my ex-husband would have me crying just like I saw him in the courtroom*, Ila thought. "Thank you, Jesus," Ila said as she got in the car with her mother.

"Maybe by the time Hampton gets out of jail he will be a changed man for sure," Ila's mother said as they drove away from the court building.

Sherre Still

We All Need to Get Away for One Reason or Another

To Ila's surprise, all of her friends had a change of heart and agreed to go on a girl's trip together. Since they had an odd number of people, Ila asked her cousin Valley to come along. Ila took it upon herself to organize the trip by contacting a travel agency to find out about the best places to take their excursion. After chatting with the travel agent, Ila got off the telephone excited that their future getaway plans were set.

"Let's see; I know Sharia and Zantaneek can't be in the same room together, so I will put Del'Feela and Sharia in one room and me and Zantaneek together and pair up Valley and Ree because they get along well with one another," Ila thought as she sent an email and text message to everyone to find out if they agreed with the room arrangements. To Ila's surprise, everyone was ok with her decision. *Shit, this is going to turn out to be a fabulous trip. Everyone agrees with every suggestion I'm sending them,* Ila thought before taking a nap.

When Ila woke up, she couldn't believe it was already 7:30. *Damn, let me get up and get going before my girls have an excuse to say why they don't have their deposit for the trip,* Ila thought. She hopped in the shower and

C' That's Why I Don't Fool with Women

lathered her body with soap to wake herself up. *I need to find me a homie lover friend,* Ila thought as she pinched her nipple with one hand and played with her clitoris with the other. After pleasing herself, Ila stepped out of the shower and prepared to get dressed. The quietness in the apartment was so odd to Ila. She was used to the telephone ringing every second of the day and it was always Hampton trying to figure out what she was doing because he wasn't there watching her and getting on her damn nerves. "THANK YOU, JESUS, FOR DELIVERING ME FROM HAMPTON'S HANDS OF EVIL," Ila screamed, not caring if her neighbors heard her rejoicing to the Lord. When Ila and Hampton separated, her family members talked about her behind her back. They thought Hampton was the breadwinner since he was a business owner, and they figured Ila wouldn't be able to make it on her own.

Ila got dressed, got her in PT Cruiser and headed to her cousin's house. When she parked and got out of the car, a few young men walked by. "Hey baby, them hips are moving the way I like," one of the young men said. Ila just kept walking toward her cousin's apartment building but kept teasing the men, switching her hips and shaking her ass.

Valley opened the door to her apartment as soon as her cousin was about to knock on the door. "Wass up, cuz! I almost didn't recognize you in that not-so-flashy car," Valley said, shutting her apartment door and eyeing her cousin from head to toe to admire the labels that she had on.

Ila walked in the kitchen to see if her cousin was cooking dinner since it was around that time, but the kitchen was clean. "Valley, you're not cooking dinner?" Ila asked.

"No, I'm not cooking dinner this evening. I have to work later tonight, and I've been up all day so all I would like to do is get a quick nap before work,".

The two ladies walked into the bedroom. Valley laid across the bed and Ila sat in the lounge chair. "Damn, excuse my manners. Would you like a glass of wine, cup of milk or ice water?" Valley teased as she sat up in bed.

Ila laughed. That was an inside joke between the two of them. When Ila and Hampton moved in together, Valley came over uninvited and Illa offered her a bottle of cold water. Valley was from the hood and felt like her cousin had changed since she had gotten her college degree, gotten married and bought a house. Valley was used to people offering her cold water from an empty milk jug in the fridge.

Sherre Still

"All I need is your deposit for the trip, so I can head to the other ladies and collect their money," Ila said.

Damn, when you asked me to go on the trip, I thought you were treating, Valley thought. "I just bought a money order to pay my rent, Ila. You don't remember me telling you that I'll pay you the deposit next week when I get paid?" Valley asked, hoping her cousin wouldn't realize she was lying.

"I don't remember what we talked about earlier. I took a nap after we got off the phone," Ila said. "I'll just pay your part of the deposit and you can pay me when you get paid."

Valley hugged her cousin. "You're the best cousin in the world," she said.

Ila left so that Valley could take a nap before work. "Aye yo yo yo baby. Are you going to give me them seven digits or what before you get in your car?" yelled a young man in the parking lot. Ila just smiled and politely got in her car without answering the young thug. As Ila drove past the young men slowly still smiling, the young man who asked for her number held up his middle finger. "Bitch," he said. He was upset about being disrespected in front of his homeboys.

C' That's Why I Don't Fool with Women

It's Time Already

The two weeks passed by so fast. It seemed like Ila had sent out the information yesterday. Ree looked through her dresser drawer to find a matching bra and panty set before putting on her jogging suit to head to the airport. Sharia was going over instructions with Wentzville to make sure the kids were taken care of while she was away. Wentzville just sat and listened as his wife went over the list for the tenth time. "Now Wentzville make sure the kids eat dinner before 6:30 p.m. and are in bed by 10 p.m.," Sharia said as she put a few more things in her suitcase.

Zantaneek stayed in her office all day patiently waiting on potential clients to come in and pay their retainer fees so that she could take as much money on the trip as possible and put some money into Pasadena's checking account. Ila was at work as well to make sure she had a full pay check once her vacation was over. Since she divorced Hampton, it wasn't hard for Ila to take charge of paying the bills and totally take care of herself.

Sherre Still

We Are on Our Way

Valley asked Ila to pick her up, so they could ride together and so that she wouldn't have to pay to park her car for four days at the airport. Ila informed Valley that a guy friend of hers was taking them to the airport so be ready when they came to pick her up. She knew Valley wasn't a punctual person. Valley assured her cousin that she would be ready, knowing that was a lie as soon as she told it.

"Now why did you just tell your cousin that you'll be ready when she gets here knowing that I have at least two more hours to finish crocheting your hair," Xlivia said as she braided Valley's hair.

Valley laughed before answering. "Because my business was none of my cousin's," she said.

Ila was grinning from ear to ear when she saw Newton's car pull up in front of her apartment complex. *Let me give a brotha points for being on time*, Ila thought as she tried to hurry up and get out of the window before Newton got out of his car and saw her. Newton got out of his Malibu standing six feet tall in his bomber leather jacket, polo sweater, blues jeans and winter boots. Jogging up the steps when he entered Ila's apartment building, Newton took a

C' That's Why I Don't Fool with Women

deep breath before pressing the doorbell. *Here goes nothing,* Ila thought as she opened the door.

"Hey Ila, how are you? Are you ready?" Newton asked as he walked into her apartment.

Damn, this man smells so freaking good! Shit, Ila thought.

"Um my luggage is over there," Ila said, wanting Newton to grab her luggage right away and take it to his car before she shut her apartment door and sexed him down before going on her trip. Ila did a walk-through of her apartment to make sure things were secure before grabbing her purse and locking the door. Newton just smiled as Ila walked his way to the car. "Damn, Ila is a nice-looking woman," he mumbled. Ila smiled back at Newton as she sat in the passenger seat, thanking him for going out of his way to take her and her cousin to the airport.

"Ila stop thanking me. I told you that it wasn't a problem when I volunteered to do it. Now tell me where your cousin lives so I get you to the airport and get back home to take a nap before work," Newton said as he started the car.

Ila gave him Valley's address and then sat quietly listening to music as her co-worker headed to pick her cousin up. *This feeling that I'm feeling feels good— to have a man wanting to do something for me for once without a motive behind it,* Ila thought as Newton pulled up at Valley's apartment complex. Ila got out of the car, praying that Valley's slow butt was ready to go. Valley's friend opened the door with a hair needle and thread in her hand.

"Hey Ila," Valley's friend said, trying to be friendly and avoid giving away the fact that Valley wasn't ready to go.

"Hey girl how you doing? Ila said, speaking to Valley's friend. She couldn't remember the woman's name.

Valley was sitting on the bed in her pajamas with a devilish smile on her face as Ila looked at her.

"Really Valley? You're not ready to go and I called before coming over here and told your black ass what time to be ready," Ila said out of anger.

"Ila don't be mad. We will be on time getting to the airport; trust me. My homegirl will be finished with my hair in about 30 minutes," Valley said, trying to calm her cousin down.

Sherre Still

"You have less than an hour to get dressed. If you're not ready, I'm leaving you," Ila said before going back outside to sit in the car with Newton.

"Newton, I'm so sorry. My cousin isn't ready to go. If she's not dressed and ready to go in an hour then you can just leave," Ila said, feeling bad that Newton had to be at work in less than four hours.

"It's not a problem. I'll just enjoy this time in the car with you," Newton said. After waiting for about 35 minutes in the car with Newton, Ila decided to go and see if Valley was just about ready to go.

"You got to be fucking kidding me, Valley," Ila said as she watched her cousin walk out of the bathroom after just taking a shower wrapped in a body towel.

Valley sat on the bed after putting on her underwear. She took her time applying lotion and getting dressed.

"Ila, now I know you didn't think I was going to get on the plane smelling funky now did you? Xlivia, put at least three pairs of socks in my suitcase and those other two outfits to the right of my closet that I bought at the boutique yesterday," Valley said. Frustrated, Ila just walked out of her cousin's apartment and headed to the car. She told Newton to just leave because her cousin wasn't ready.

As Newton started the engine, Valley came running to his car with her luggage in hand. Being a gentleman, Newton put Valley's luggage in the trunk while she got in the car. "Enjoy your trip," Xlivia said as Valley got in her car. Ila was mad as hell at her cousin for not being ready. *C that's why I don't fool with women because a lot of the time they can be a mess*, Ila thought.

Since Ila wouldn't formally introduce Valley to her male friend, she took it upon herself to do so. "Since my cousin is being rude, my name is Valley and your name is?" Valley asked politely.

"My name is Newton. Pleased to meet you," he said, not wanting to get in between the female drama seeing that Ila was clearly upset with her family member.

By the time they arrived at the airport, it was so crowded that Ila just knew they weren't going to make it to the departure gate to get out of town. *Luggage needs to be checked and then we must go through the security check*, Ila thought as she stared at the people standing in the long line. Newton

C' That's Why I Don't Fool with Women

helped the ladies with their luggage and told them to have a good time in New York City. He gave Ila a friendly hug and slipped a $100 bill in her pocket.

"Newton, you don't have to give me any money. Giving us a ride and offering to be back at the airport to pick us up is enough," Ila said, trying to give Newton the money back.

"Hey, Newton I'll take the money if my cousin won't take it," Valley said in a serious tone.

"Shut the hell up," Ila whispered as she put the money back in her pocket and gave Newton a friendly hug before grabbing her luggage.

Ila and Valley went through the security check, put their shoes back on and ran to the departure gate. *If we don't get on this damn plane because of Valley I'm not fooling with her ass no mo*, Ila thought as she and her cousin kept running. Once they arrived at gate 42, Ila couldn't believe that Ree, Zantaneek, Sharia and Del'Feela were waiting for them. They thought something must have happened to Ila because she wasn't answering her phone, and they didn't want to leave her behind.

"Ila girl, what happened? We been have calling your cellphone for the past 20 minutes," Ree said worried.

"I don't even want to talk about it," Ila said. Relieved that they didn't waste their money, the ladies boarded the plane, sat down and went to sleep.

Before they knew it, the flight was over. "Ladies and gentlemen, I would like to welcome you to New York. Please wait until the plane lands to release your seat belt," the pilot said.

Valley reached in the row in front of her to wake Ila up, who was snoring from being so tired after working right up until it was time to leave for the trip. The ladies got their luggage and then headed to the rental terminal to get the minivan they reserved. After loading up, Sharia volunteered to drive. She ran her mouth about visiting New York City when she was younger on family vacations. *Bah bah bah,* Zantaneek thought as she listened to Sharia go on and on. By the time they arrived at the hotel, all Ila could think about was getting her money from Valley. She didn't have too much to say to her cousin. While the other ladies were giving their information to the desk clerk in the hotel, Ila pulled Valley aside to have a private conversation. "Valley when are you going to give me the money for the trip because I need some spending money," Ila said, feeling a bit stupid asking for money that was owed to her.

"Ila as soon as I get settled in the room with Ree I will call and check my direct deposit. If it did, we can go to an ATM machine, so I can give you your money," Valley said as though she had an attitude about her cousin even asking for her money. Ila was getting a bad vibe from Valley. Ila took the high road and just walked away with Zantaneek and left Valley waiting on Ree.

C' That's Why I Don't Fool with Women

Getting Settled in the Room

"So, what's going on Ila?" Zantaneek asked, sensing that something was wrong.
"Aww, nothing much. Valley and I had to straighten something out is all," Ila said, not wanting to discuss the matter and get all upset. To relieve some stress, Ila took a pill to kill the anxiety. After putting her clothes in the closet and taking a shower, Zantaneek and Ila both decided to take a nap, so they could be ready for the night life. At 6:45 p.m. there was a knock at Zantaneek and Ila's door. "I want to sleep at least one more hour before we get going," Zantaneek said, covering her head with the pillow when Ila asked her to get up.
"One more hour, Ila. We aren't in a rush to go anywhere while on vacation. It feels good to not have an appointed time to be someplace," Zantaneek said as her friend agreed with her, covering her head up with the pillow.
Within 10 minutes there was another knock at the door. Ila got up out of bed to answer the door, because she wanted the knocking to stop. As soon as Ila turned the knob and pulled the door open, Sharia, Del'Feela and Ree said,

Sherre Still

"Are y'all ready to have fun?" Valley was standing back looking at them act a fool.

"Y'all c'mon in here before we all get put out of the hotel," Ila said laughing at her friends.

Ree, Sharia, Del'Feela and Valley all said that they would be waiting at the hotel bar downstairs while Ila and Zantaneek got dressed. It was no fun sitting in a room looking at each other while waiting on someone to get dressed when they could be having drinks and listening to music instead.

"Zantaneek, get your ass up so that we can join the party people," Ila said, looking in the closet trying to decide which outfit she wanted to wear.

Reluctantly, Zantaneek got out of bed after Ila kept making noises to keep her from sleeping. Before leaving St. Louis, Zantaneek and Mantha got into a horrible argument about the awful things that were posted on social media. Feeling bad and somewhat depressed, Zantaneek wanted to call her spoiled rotten daughter and say she was sorry for calling her a selfish bitch but then thought, *no I'm going to enjoy my trip*. Within minutes, Zantaneek had gotten dressed and was walking out of the door with Ila ready to have a good time.

Once at the hotel bar, the women popped their fingers to the music and cheered some Caucasian man on as he danced with Del'Feela, who was tooting her butt toward him on the dance floor. Zantaneek and Ila decided to go to the bar. As soon as the ladies sat down, a waitress took their order. When she came back with the drinks, she told them the drinks were paid for by the man dancing with Del'Feela. Since they were drinking on someone else's tab, Valley took advantage by ordering the most expensive drink with double shots each time the waitress came by. Since the ladies were having such a great time at the bar inside the hotel, they all decided to stay since the Caucasian gentleman was a true sweetheart.

C' That's Why I Don't Fool with Women

Recover

The next morning Valley was sick as a dog and throwing up. Ree decided to call Ila to come and see about her cousin because she didn't feel like tending to Valley as if she was at work instead of being on a mini vacation. When Ree called Ila, Ila simply stated that she wasn't coming to Valley's rescue until she got her money. *Damn*, Ree thought after hanging up the telephone. *C that's why I don't fool with women, family members included, because they can be a trip. I would have had to whoop Valley's ass certainly for trying to play me*, Ree thought. Ree ordered breakfast so that she could eat before the day got started with the ladies. Within 15 minutes, Ree's breakfast was delivered and she enjoyed it before Valley came out of the bathroom and walked slowly to the bed to rest.

"Ree, do you mind calling my cousin to let her know that I'm staying in for the day, because I'm not feeling good," Valley said, laying her head on the pillow because her head was spinning. Ree didn't reply. She just went to the bathroom to take a shower so that she could get dressed and out of Valley's presence.

Sherre Still

Ila was pleased when she found out through Ree that Valley couldn't join them for the day. Their first stop was the sex museum. All the ladies enjoyed doing the activities together, acting like teenagers as they laughed and joked with one another. Their next stop was the wax museum, because it was as close to some of the celebrities any of the ladies would ever get. The ladies took photos with their favorite celebrity wax figures, laughing and joking around and really enjoying the moment.

While Sharia and Zantaneek took more pictures, Ree and Ila walked away from the crowd to talk. "Do you want me to suggest to your cousin that she needs to give you your money?" Ree asked, trying to help.

"No, I decided that if she doesn't give me my money then I'm going to stop dealing with her. As I told you this morning, if I hadn't paid Valley's fee for the trip it would have been three to one room and two to the other with a person being upset about paying more money than was expected. Ree, you don't get along with a lot of people so there's no way I was going to have you share a room with one of my friends that you're not really cool with and something bad kick off and then I feel bad about it," Ila said.

Seeing that the other ladies were coming their way, all Ree could do was fall back and mind her business by continuing to enjoy herself and just see how things turned out.

"Well let's enjoy the trip and not stress," Ree said with a wink as they walked out of the building.

"Let's go shopping at the Alley," Sharia suggested. Since Sharia was determined to shop at the Alley, which was like a swap meet or flea market, they went there next to shut her up. They were all glad they went, because they all found great bargains.

"Damn, I hope I don't have to buy another suitcase to take my things back home, because last time I traveled I did and another time I had to pay $75 because my suitcase was overloaded," Ree said, giving all the ladies something to think about as they shopped.

"I say we not go shopping no more while we're here and we just keep sight-seeing and partying because Ree brought up a good point," Zantaneek said as Ree volunteered to drive back to the hotel.

As Ree pulled out of the parking lot, everyone said, "I thought her ass was sick." They saw Valley walking to the cab with several shopping bags. Ila was

C' That's Why I Don't Fool with Women

pissed. "Give that bitch time to get back to the hotel. I want to see if Valley even tells me she left the room," Ila said as Ree drove the long route going back to the hotel.

"Bitch! Watch where you're going," a road rage driver said, passing Ree. Ree was pissed because she wasn't in the wrong, so she caught up with the driver and gave him the middle finger.

"Girl are you crazy or what? I got a family that I want to go back home to," Sharia said, scared half to death of what Ree had just done.

"That bastard almost hit us when I had the right of way. Then he called me a bitch on top of that. Fuck that asshole," Ree said as she continued driving toward the hotel.

"Well Ms. Mighty Ree, the road rage driver is following us since you gave him the middle finger. These people here in New York don't play," Del'Feela said.

Zantaneek took a picture of the road rage driver's license plate so that she could give it to the police after whatever happened, if they survived the ordeal. Ree pulled over, because she didn't want the driver to know where they were staying.

"Ila, if the driver pulls out a weapon and shoots me, drive off and call the police," Ree said, not wanting them all to get harmed.

"Girl, I'm not going to let you get out of the car by yourself. We came on this trip together so I'm getting out of the van with you," Ila said.

Del'Feela, Zantaneek and Sharia didn't feel the one-for-all and all-for-what-Ila-thought-was-one. "Ree keep the engine on when you and Ila get out of the van. I'll drive away and call the police when I arrive to the hotel," Del'Feela said, just keeping things real. She wasn't ready to meet her maker if she had the option.

Ree hopped out of the van and left the engine running. Ila tried to open the passenger door, but Zantneek held her back.

"Ila, you have been through too much stupid shit with Hampton for me to watch you lose your life on a trip with a friend of yours, not mine, doing the craziest thing in the world," Zantaneek said as Ila turned off the van engine, refusing to leave Ree behind.

The road rage driver turned out to be a woman who was the size of a wrestler. She got out of the car cussing and calling Ree every profane name that you could think of, trying to get a fight started. Ree's heart was beating so fast. She couldn't believe the size of the female as she got even closer to her. As the woman approached Ree, Ree had to think fast before things got physical. Ree hit the back of the minivan and began throwing her hands up in the air like a crazy woman, trying to get out the words she was trying to say. "Ain't this a bitch," the road rage driver said. "I can't fight a person with a disability. This bitch can't talk. She's deaf. You're lucky I got a bit of sympathy for your non-hearing ass, because my momma has the same disability," the road rage driver said before getting back in her car, thinking that the other ladies in the van were deaf as well.

Relieved, Ree got back in the van and told Sharia to get behind the wheel. Ree was done driving in New York City. The ladies laughed until they cried just thinking about Ree's performance. "Ree, you missed your calling. You should have been a comedian instead of a nurse because you are acting a fool for real," Ila said wiping the tears from her eyes.

The ladies fell silent when they got to the hotel, not knowing what was going to happen between Ila and her cousin. Sharia said a silent prayer as she parked, hoping nobody would get locked up on their vacation. To everyone's surprise, Ila headed toward her hotel room and Zantaneek followed behind her, surprised she wasn't going to Ree and Valley's hotel room down the hallway.

"What time are we to be ready for tonight?" Sharia asked before going into her hotel room.

"Ila said we should be ready to go around 9:00," Zantaneek said before shutting the hotel room door.

Ree walked into her hotel room surprised to see Valley in the bed with her pajamas on watching television as though she never left the room. *This bitch is an actress,* Ree thought as she tried to keep her composure.

"How was the outing in the N.Y.C?" Valley asked, thanking God that she had made it back in time before anyone ever knew she left the hotel.

Before answering Valley's question, Ree looked around the hotel room for evidence that she had left the hotel room. On the opposite side of the bed there it was, the same shopping bags everyone saw Valley carrying to the cab.

C' That's Why I Don't Fool with Women

"Ah our outing seeing the N.Y.C. was an experience. So, tell me how your outing was. We saw you out Valley with those shopping bags from the flea market that you're hiding on the side of the bed," Ree said with an attitude.

Shit, if Ree saw me out at the flea market then that means the rest of the ladies saw me as well, Valley thought trying to think of something to say. Valley's plan was to have all of the items she had purchased in her suitcase before Ree returned to the hotel room.

"Ah… ah…," was all Valley could say, being lost for words.

"Ah it's a shame how you played your cousin by not giving her money for financing the trip. Payback is a you know what, Valley. If you didn't have all of the funds, you could have at least given Ila a partial payment! Damn," Ree said, taking her shoes off before laying across the bed to take a nap.

Ree's comment hit home, making Valley really feel bad about not paying Ila back. *Shid, Ila has money. She know damn well I don't make as much money at the factory as she does working as a nurse*, Valley thought before taking a nap to be ready to go out for the night.

Sherre Still

It's Time to Party

"It's time to get ready and par'tay! Get off the phone and start getting ready, Sharia," Del'Feela said while drying off after taking a shower. Sharia ignored Del'Feela's comment about getting dressed because she was wondering where in the hell her husband and children were at that time of night. He should have been feeding the kids and preparing to give them a bath before bed. After calling home with still no answer, Sharia was pissed off. She turned her cell phone off and got ready to head out.

Ila and Zantaneek were dressed and ready to go, dancing to the music until their friends called to say they were ready to leave. "You're looking cute tonight Ila," Zantaneek said, admiring Ila's fat ass.

Ila had to turn around and look at Zantaneek like she was crazy, knowing she always looked her best. "Girl what are you talking about? I look good every time I go out," Ila said before turning back to the mirror to finish applying her makeup. When Ree called Zantaneek to let her know they were ready, they all agreed to meet at the hotel bar in 10 minutes.

Ree and Valley's ride on the elevator was quiet, with Valley basically talking to herself. *Can't she see that we ain't got nothing to talk about,* Ree

C' That's Why I Don't Fool with Women

thought as she walked off of the elevator with Valley still running her mouth as though they were having a decent conversation. Del'Feela and Sharia were already having drinks at the bar when Ree and Valley arrived.

"What's up girlie?" Sharia said to Ree, who turned around in slow motion so that everyone could get a good look at her outfit.

Anybody can buy a basic spandex dress. This chic thinks she got it going on. The only thing she has on are those nice ass shoes, Del'Feela thought as she said, "Hey Ree, that's a nice outfit."

Valley sat at the bar and got the bartender's attention. She needed a drink to ignore the bad vibe amongst the women. Within five minutes, Zantaneek and Ila appeared at the bar ready to have a drink and get going. "Hey Valley," Ila said as she sat down beside her to order a drink.

"Hey cuz," Valley said while analyzing her cousin's outfit. Ila was sporting a long sleeve romper with a pair of tight tall boots that showcased her shapely legs. All the ladies laughed and drank until they all agreed that it was time to get going to par'tay. The valet pulled their rental van around to the front door of the hotel and Ila tipped the gentleman while everyone got inside.

"Ah excuse me Valley, but ah I don't think you were invited on this outing or anything else for the rest of this trip," Ila said.

Damn, I didn't see this coming, the ladies thought. Valley had never been so embarrassed in her life by a family member. This was Ila's way of paying Valley back for not repaying her the money.

"Ila, you gon sit up here and try to embarrass me in front of your so-called friends, bitch," Valley said, pissed off.

Del'Feela, Ree, Zantaneek and Sharia looked at Valley and then back at Ila after hearing that comment, trying to figure out what it meant. Ila was now angry enough to fight since Valley was trying her best to totally ruin her trip with her friends. With a quick leap, Ila came out of the driver's seat and charged into Valley in the back seat.

"Who you calling a bitch, heffa?" Ila said with a punch to her cousin's face.

"Kick her ass Ila," all her friends said, being on her side.

Valley broke away from Ila's grip to get out of the van. "You are going to get what's coming to you Ila," Valley said as a tear fell from her eye before going back into the hotel.

Sherre Still

Before Ila could drive away from the hotel, Ree told her friend to wait so she could take care of something right fast. Seeing Valley had gone inside of the bar instead of going back to the hotel room, Ree went to the front desk to ask that the keys to her room be changed so that Valley could no longer enter. Quickly, Ree went to the hotel room to get Valley's suitcase to sit it outside of the door. *That bitch is going to be mad*, Ree thought as she headed back downstairs.

"Let's go and kick it," Ree said, dancing beside the van before getting inside.

After consuming as many drinks as she could handle, Valley politely declined the Caucasian man's offer to go to his room for a night cap. *I guess I'm on my own for the rest of the trip*, Valley thought as she walked down the hallway noticing her luggage sitting outside of the hotel room.

"What the fuck is my luggage doing sitting out in the hallway," Valley said mad as hell as she inserted her hotel key in the slot trying to unlock the door.

Really pissed off now, Valley went to the front desk to find out what the problem was. Ree told management that the person sharing the room with her didn't pay her fee so she wanted to change the keys so the other party wouldn't be able to enter the room. Since the room was in Ree's name, management did as she asked and didn't get into a deep conversation with Valley when she got loud in the lobby.

The next morning, the ladies all laughed at Zantaneek's dance performance at the club. "Let us see your ass get up on this table like you did last night Z," Ila said, kidding around with her friend laughing.

Zantaneek laughed with the ladies but refused to hop on the table like she did when she was drunk the night before.

"Hey y'all, after we all get through eating breakfast do you all mind finding a nail spa around someplace, so I can get a manicure and pedicure?" Sharia asked with a smile.

The ladies kept eating and kept their thoughts to themselves. *C that's why I don't fool with women. Who in the fuck goes on a trip and uses the limited time to do something that they could very well do at home?* Ree thought.

Hell, naw we ain't going to a nail spa on our last day in the N.Y.C., Ila thought as she continued to eat her breakfast. The ladies finished breakfast and then enjoyed a day of sightseeing.

C' That's Why I Don't Fool with Women

Returning Home

Valley ended up staying at a shabby motel with the funds she had. It took no time for Valley to take a hoe bath and get dressed so that she could catch a cab to the airport. *It's a good thing Ila gave me the information to check in for my flight or I bet she would have been petty about that too*, Valley thought.

Feeling good that the rest of the trip wasn't a disaster, Ila was glad the ladies were cordial with one another and they all got along. As the ladies walked together to their departure gate, they wondered if Valley would be there ready to get back to Saint Louis to tell everybody what happened to her in the N.Y.C. *Bitches*, Valley thought as she looked at Ila and her friends looking at her like they were surprised to see her. As the ladies took their seats on the plane, they couldn't wait to get home.

Once Ree heard the pilot announce that they had arrived in Saint Louis, she nudged Ila so that she could wake up. Valley couldn't wait to get off the plane so that she could get home and tell the family how Ila treated her when they were out of town. Sharia was one of the first passengers of the group to get off the plane. She couldn't wait to hear Wentzville's speech about why he was missing while she away. All the ladies hugged one another after gathering their luggage and then went their separate ways to go home. Wentzville pulled up curbside when his wife walked out of the airport. *At least Wentzville came to pick me up on time,* Sharia thought smiling at her husband as he got out of the car to give her a bear hug and get her luggage.

"Hey baby! How was your trip? We missed you while you were away," Wentzville said, giving Sharia a kiss on cheek. Sharia had to play nice with her husband in front of her girlfriends because she didn't want them to know her personal business. As soon as they got inside of the car and drove away from the airport, Sharia let Wentzville have it.

"MOTHER FUCK'CA DON'T YOU 'HEY HONEY' ME. HOW WAS MY DAMN TRIP? WHERE IN THE HELL HAVE YOU BEEN WENTZVILLE NOT BEING ABLE TO ANSWER MY DAMN CALLS?" Sharia screamed.

Wentzville knew he was in trouble with his wife, but he didn't think she was going to be bitching as soon as she got inside of the car. "Sharia, I had to work while you were away, and my mother watched the kids since I worked a double shift," Wentzville lied.

Sharia knew she and Wentzville had been having marital problems for a while, but she didn't think it would get this bad. "Wentzville, why lie to me of all people? I know for a fact that you weren't at work and that you left the kids at your mother's house the entire time I was away. Who in the fuck did you take to the movie theater and then out to eat and then withdraw $200 from our bank account for?" Sharia asked with a straight face as they sat at a red light.

How in the hell does Sharia know every move I made while she was out of town? Wentzville wondered. He was speechless. Sharia was very upset because Wentzville hadn't come up with an answer, so she slapped him as hard as she could to get him to say something.

"You don't have anything to say Wentzville?" Sharia asked in tears, being so upset knowing that her husband was being unfaithful yet again.

"Sharia, it's not what you think; trust me please," Wentzville pleaded, knowing Sharia knew that he had been stepping outside of the marriage once more. It was something about a woman working a 9 to 5 that turned Wentzville on. Every time Wentzville would suggest Sharia get a least a part-

C' That's Why I Don't Fool with Women

time job, Sharia said that she wanted to stay home and nurture their children until they entered high school.

"Wentzville, I want your dumb ass to move out of the house today till you decide on what you want out of this life that we have together. Our bank account shows every move that you make when using your bank card that I, as your wife, have access to. The week before I left to go out of town, you used your bank card to go to dinner. Then I checked your pockets before doing the laundry and found the receipt for the motel across the street from the restaurant where you used the bank card on that same day within the same time frame. I hate your trifling ass," Sharia said getting out of the car when she saw her mother-in-law walk out on the porch of their home with their children.

Wentzville rubbed his goatee out of shame. He was ashamed that his wife electronically checked him out creeping with his young whore. Getting out of the car and walking slowly behind his wife, Wentzville was thinking he better get his shit together before he was out of the house permanently and paying alimony and child support.

Del'Feela took a deep breath before turning the key in the lock of her mother's home, praying that there be no drama as soon as she walked inside. *Damn, it's dark in here. I know momma isn't asleep this early in the day,* Del'Feela thought as she walked to her mother's bedroom. There she found her crackhead brother going through the dresser drawer looking for something valuable to pawn. "What the hell are you doing going through momma's dresser drawers Luke?" Del'Feela asked, dropping her luggage on the floor.

"Ah ah momma sent me over here to get her some more underwear because she ran out of clean clothes," Luke lied. Luke was feeling sick to his stomach and wanting to find anything of value so that he could get going to make some money to feed his addiction.

"Where's momma at?" Del'Feela asked, wondering where in the hell her mother could be since she wasn't at home.

"Momma is at Baptisia's house, because you went on your trip. No one was home to feed momma and get her ready for her doctor's appointments," Luke said while still going through his mother's drawers trying to find something to steal. Del'Feela was pissed because she had paid her sister Tarsila to take care of their mother while she was away.

Sherre Still

"Luke give me your key to the house, and I don't want your thieving ass around here anymore or I'm calling the police on your black ass," Del'Feela said, reaching out for his house key. Luke threw the house key to Del'Feela, cussing her out as he went out of the front door. Del'Feela held up her middle finger and told her brother to kiss her black ass before slamming the front door behind him. Del'Feela went through her purse looking for her cellphone so that she could locate this dude she used to deal with to change the locks before she headed over to her sister Baptisia's house to get her mother.

Ila was so happy to be back home to try to begin a new relationship with Newton. "Ila, I didn't realize you had a mean bone in your body until you dissed your cousin at the airport. You could have at least allowed me to take the woman home. Damn, girl," Newton said laughing.

"Yes, I could have but I didn't because my cousin Valley broke the 'I'm going to pay you back' code so that's what she gets in return — no more damn favors from me. What was most insulting about the situation was she was spending money in my face knowing that she hadn't paid me back," Ila said laughing before taking a sip of her drink.

"I know babe, but ah you pissed your cousin off when we left her behind at the airport," Newton said as he got closer to Ila on the couch and hoped for a little kiss.

Zantaneek walked in the house and couldn't believe how badly her house was trashed. Mantha had a party every day while her mother was away on her girl's trip. *What the fuck*, Zantaneek thought as she walked inside of her home and kicked the beer bottles and cans out of the way. Zantaneek pushed the door open and walked into the kitchen to find a me'nage a trois going down in the middle of the floor. Two white girls were playing with each other's nipples as they kissed one another while the black boy enjoyed savaging one of the white girls and fucking the other as she rode him. "Get the hell out of my house now, or I'll call the police," Zantaneek said as calmly as she could.

The two white girls and the black boy that was hung like a horse hurried up and gathered their clothes to run out of the back door of the house. Mantha was shocked to see her mother standing before her in the kitchen as she was smoking a blunt and styling in her mother's lingerie.

"What in the world are you doing in my lingerie Mantha?" Zantaneek asked, walking up on her daughter with a disgusted look on her face.

C' That's Why I Don't Fool with Women

"I really wasn't expecting you back home so soon mother," Mantha said, putting the blunt out on one of Zantaneek's expensive pieces of China. Zantaneek reached to snatch a hand full of daughter's hair but Mantha ran out of the kitchen before her mother could get ahold of her.

Ree smiled as her husband delivered a welcome home kiss to the lower half of her body. With a flick of Falcon's wrist and the twiddle of his finger, he licked Ree's kitty as she moaned with pleasure. She was in lust heaven with her man.

Once Del'Feela got the dude she used to mess around with to change the locks to the front and back door of her mother's house so that her siblings could no longer get in, she headed over to her sister's house. *Please let this be a pleasant visit. I just want to get momma in my car and go home without cussing this bitch Baptisia out,* Del'Feela thought as she knocked on her sister's front door.

"Who is it?" Baptisia shouted, not expecting anyone for a visit.

"It's me, Del'Feela," she replied. Baptisia let her sister inside. She had an attitude because she was jealous that her sister had just returned from a trip she could never afford. "Hey Baptisia, that no-good ass brother of ours said momma is over here. Is that true?" Del'Feela asked, seeming really concerned to know their mother whereabouts.

Baptisia put her hands on her wide hips. "Yeah momma's here with me and been here ever since you went on your girl's vacation with her social security check to enjoy yourself," she said.

Del'Feela gave her sister a look. If looks could kill, Baptisia sure enough would have been dead. *Let me get momma and get the fuck out of Baptisia's house before we get to fighting up in here. And I can't wait to see that other no-good ass sister of mine. She's giving me my money back I paid her to take care of momma,* Del'Feela thought as she walked in the living room where she knew her momma would be. Manwella was watching the 5:00 news when Del'Feela walked in the living room.

"Hey momma," Del'Feela said.

"Hey Del'Feela! I'm glad you're back. I'm ready to go home where the hell I live at," Manwella said while trying to reach for her house shoes to put them on right away.

Sherre Still

Manwella told Del'Feela that Baptisia had gone to the casino without her since she didn't have any money and mistreated her, knowing she needed assistance getting dressed before going to adult daycare. The whole time Manwella was talking, Del'Feela felt anxiety come over her and wondered why in the hell she had to come back home to the bullshit. "So, you are telling me you didn't eat today and it's almost 6:00 momma?" Del'Feela asked. Her mother was diabetic and needed to eat at least three meals a day so that her sugar wouldn't drop.

"Like I said, I didn't eat nothing today," Manwella said.

Del'Feela walked past Baptisia to get the bag of food she had picked up on the way home from the airport. She decided to heat it up for her mother to eat before taking her home. Baptisia walked into the room to speak what was on her mind because she was tired of her mother lying on her.

"I don't know why you're believing momma didn't eat anything because you should know that she did. I'm diabetic just like momma and know damn well she needs to eat at least two meals a day. Now, I might not cook what momma wants to eat at the time but that's her problem if she refuses to eat it. When momma gets her social security check or her food stamps next month I need for you to buy a bottle of ketchup and a five-pound bag of sugar because momma ate all of mine up and denied it when I asked her about it," Baptisia said before going upstairs to her bedroom where her boyfriend was watching television.

Manwella followed behind Del'Feela, who asked her to come to the kitchen while she heated up her food. "Your sister is a dirty dog; I'm telling you, Del'Feela. When my momma and papa was living, we wouldn't dare treat them like Baptisia treats me," Manwella said while waiting for the food to warm up.

Del'Feela ignored her mother's comment because she played one child against the other when she couldn't get her way. As Del'Feela opened the oven door to get a skillet out, she saw a large bottle of ketchup and a five-pound bag a sugar hidden inside behind the pots and pans. *This bitch has a lot of nerve to request that I buy anything that she said momma has eaten up when it's hidden right here in her oven,* Del'Feela thought. After Del'Feela heated up the food for her mother, she reached inside of the oven to get the ketchup bottle and handed it over to her mother and then took the bag of sugar

C' That's Why I Don't Fool with Women

out to make some homemade lemonade. Manwella went straight to eating after putting ketchup all over her food without even praying, proving that she was hungry. After taking a few bites of her sandwich Manwella said, "I told you your sister can be a dirty dog. Baptisia had ketchup and sugar hidden and told me that she had ran out and needed to buy some more because I ate it all up. She wouldn't have told that lie to that good-for-nothing nigga she got upstairs in her bedroom that sleeps over here almost every night. That nigga is going to use Baptisia all the way up and throw her away like trash once he finds another stupid woman with more than her to use and abuse."

Del'Feela encouraged her mother to hurry up and eat so they could get going back home because she had better things to do than sit in her sister's home where she felt she was never welcome. As soon as Baptisia heard the front door close, she went downstairs, relieved that her mother was finally gone back home so that she could have some peace and quiet. When Baptisia walked in the kitchen she read the note Del'Feela left behind.

Baptisia, you can be so petty at times to try your best to piss people off. Who in the world would hide ketchup and sugar in the oven to keep their momma from having some? Your lying ass would. Next time leave her at home, bitch.

Your sista only by blood not relation,
Del'Feela

Baptisia balled up the note and threw it in the trash before going back upstairs to cater to her man.

As soon as Del'Feela got her mother situated at home, she took a shower to relieve some stress and then got in bed. "This feels so good to be in bed. I pray momma doesn't call my name for nothing tonight," Del'Feela said before closing her eyes and dreading going to work in the morning.

Just as she was about to drift off to sleep, the phone rang. *Shit,* Del'Feela thought. "Hello," she said.

"Hey, Del'Feela. How was the girl's trip," Pasadena asked, ready to hear the gossip.

Del'Feela really didn't want to talk about the trip but told her cousin all about it anyway. "You should have been there to see the family feud go down between Ila and her cousin Valley. We knew nothing really about what was going on between Ila and her cousin until the bitch played sick and went shopping on her own. We saw her on our outing while we were sightseeing," Del'Feela said, going on and on about the trip.

That's not what Pasadena really wanted to know. "That's crazy, Del'Feela," she said. "So how did Zantaneek carry herself on the trip? Did she meet anyone?" Pasadena asked, hoping the answer was no so that she wouldn't have to end her conversation with Del'Feela to call and straighten Zantaneek's ass out.

"Girl, Zantaneek was on her best behavior and not interested in trying to meet anyone. Zantaneek talked about her daughter and them getting into it before leaving but that conversation was brief, because we were trying to leave the Saint Louis troubles behind until we got back home," Del'Feela said.

Pasadena was satisfied with that answer, so she moved on. "So, have you heard from your boo since he has been on lock down?" she asked, wanting to know if her cousin had been in touch with her secret lover.

"No, I haven't heard from him since he called me saying that his lawyer would be in touch with me soon to put money on his books,"

"Well, I'm going to suggest you make sure that no one finds out about your secret affair with the convict and that we are related, or your friends are going to be scorned certainly," Del'Feela assured her cousin that no one was going to find out anything because she didn't share all her personal business with friends.

"So, tell me about your girlfriend trip," Xlivia said ready to hear some gossip. Valley couldn't wait to tell the story to anyone who was willing to listen to her side.

"That bitch ass cousin of mine treated me like a step-child when we got to New York City. I had to stay at a motel because her so-called friend Ree kicked me out of the room that she and I were sharing,".

"What the fuck did you just say?" Xlivia asked, not believing what her friend on a good day just said.

"You heard me, Xlivia. The bitch kicked me out of the room that we were sharing because it was in her name," Valley said.

After listening to the entire story, Xlivia figured something just didn't sound right so she asked a valid question that would make sense of everything. "Something just don't sound right, Valley. Why in the world would your cousin allow a friend to disrespect you when you clearly stated

C' That's Why I Don't Fool with Women

that you all didn't get into it with one another? I would have had to kick your cousin's ass and her friend Ree's ass too if I had paid my hard-earned money and she disrespected me,"

Glad that her friend agreed that Ila deserved what was coming to her, Valley continued running her mouth, being all hyped up.

"That's why I'm not going to pay her a dime back for the trip to New York City since she did what she did. Ila should have gotten her motherfucking money first before I got on the plane. Ya feel me?" Valley said. She was cracking up laughing so hard that she didn't realize Xlivia wasn't laughing with her.

When Xlivia crocheted Valley's hair to go on her trip to New York City, she had just gotten off from her 9 to 5. With a sincere promise, Valley vowed to pay Xlivia back once she returned to Saint Louis. After hearing Valley admit that she hadn't paid for her trip to New York at all, Xlivia understood why her friend on any good day went through what she experienced. "Valley, you are something else. You called me to listen to your story playing the victim. Have my money ready for me to pick up for doing your hair in about an hour," Xlivia said before hanging up the telephone.

As Xlivia got dressed to go pick up her money from Valley, she said to herself, "C that's why I don't fool with women."

Sherre Still

Taking an Additional Day Off from Work

Ree smiled as she drove over to her grandmother's apartment building to pay her a surprise visit. As normal, no one was sitting in the lobby to let Ree into her grandmother's apartment building. Crossing her fingers and praying someone was in the management office, Ree pressed in the code with hopes of getting in the building right away. "May I help you?" the office manager asked through the intercom.

Ree shivered as she talked. "Yes, this is Ms. Mary-Lee's granddaughter. Can you let me in please?" she asked.

The office manager buzzed Ree into the senior citizen apartment building and then came out in the hallway to meet her. "How are you doing? I forgot your name, but I do remember your grandmother introducing you to me. What is your name again?" Ms. Curtain asked.

"Thanks for letting me in the building. My name is Ree," she said.

"Can I have a moment of your time in my office please?" Ms. Curtain asked, not wanting their conversation to be overheard. Ree followed Ms. Curtain into her office, wondering why she wanted to have a one-on-one. "Ree, we had an issue the other day in your grandmother's apartment. She let

C' That's Why I Don't Fool with Women

the tub overflow and the water went into the apartment underneath hers. This is only a suggestion, but I believe your grandmother needs to be seen by a doctor because something doesn't seem right with her. Your grandmother denied letting her tub overflow, but we could clearly see it had," Ms. Curtain said, hoping Ms. Mary-Lee's granddaughter would take her to the doctor and find out the problem so they wouldn't have to evict her.

Ree told Ms. Curtain that she was a nurse and thanked her for her concerns. *Grandma probably overslept and let the tub overflow and that's why she probably denied it. She was ashamed that she did that,* Ree thought as she walked down the hallway to her grandmother's apartment. After knocking two times, Ree heard her grandmother's voice through the door.

"Who is it?" Mary-Lee asked.

"It's me grandma," Ree said, praying her grandmother's apartment didn't feel like a hot August day when she walked inside.

Mary-Lee opened the apartment door. "Hey baby, what brings you to my neck of the woods?" Mary-Lee asked as she sat at the kitchen table in her bra and granny panties about to eat some corn bread and collard greens.

"I just wanted to see you and tell you about my trip with my girlfriends," Ree said. Her grandmother offered her supper, but Ree wasn't hungry. *Let me turn this heat down to 74 degrees and turn off the oven. It feels like a fucking sauna up in here*, Ree thought as she adjusted the temperature. Then she went to the bathroom to check for evidence of the tub overflowing. *Lord have mercy,* Ree thought as she flushed the toilet and turned off the water that was running from the faucet. As Ree turned around and looked at the closet door, she could see wet towels piled up that smelled of mold. "Grandma, I need you to go somewhere with me after you eat," Ree said as though they were just going for a ride.

"Where you going? I don't feel like going anyplace," Mary-Lee said as she continued to eat with her fingers, enjoying her food. Ree made up a lie to get her grandmother to get up and get dressed so that she could take her to the emergency room to be seen by a doctor.

As Ree and her grandmother sat in the emergency room, Mary-Lee asked at least 20 times where they were and why they were there. Because Ree had a lot of patience, she answered each question until the nurse called her grandmother's name. The doctor ordered labs, an MRI and a CT scan and discovered that Mary-Lee had a slight touch of dementia. Ree's heart sank because that was the last thing she wanted to hear. She took her grandmother home with her and knew she had to do everything in her power to keep her loved one going strong. "Grandma come on and let me help you out of the car," Ree said.

"Who lives here?" Mary-Lee asked as they rode the elevator.

"Grandma, I live here and you're going to stay with me for a little while," Ree said as she unlocked her apartment door. Ree got her grandmother settled in her bedroom and then called her mother to talk about a future care plan for her grandmother. "Well Ree you know momma ain't going to go for no adult daycare," Violet said.

Ree heard her mother, but still wanted to give it a try. The next day she visited a few adult daycares and filled out FMLA paperwork at work to get some leave approved. As though she was at work, Ree took care of her grandmother by feeding her, bathing her and then putting her to bed as though she was one of her patients.

"Grandma, I love you," Ree said as she rubbed and kissed her grandmother's forehead.

C' That's Why I Don't Fool with Women

We're Having a Guest Stay with Us Awhile

    Just when Del'Feela thought things couldn't get any worse, her ex-lover called the day after she got back from New York City. "Baby, I just want you to know that I'm sorry for what I said and did, and I want to know if you can help your boy out," Quail said, hoping Del'Feela would come to his rescue.
    "What is it Q?" Del'Feela asked, as though she wasn't going to assist.
    "Ah you see ah ah. I'm in need of a place to stay as of today because I didn't renew my lease and want to know if I can stay at yo momma crib," Quail said, trying to make Del'Feela feel sorry for a brotha. Del'Feela had to really think about the question, because she didn't want to be bothered with a male negro on a daily basis.
    "A couple of days Q?" Del'Feela asked to make sure he was asking only for a few days. Del'Feela gave in and told Quail that he could stay until the end of the week, giving him more than enough time to find another place to live. After getting the ok that he could camp out at Del'Feela's momma's crib, Quail asked Del'Feela to pick him up because his transmission went out in his car. Del'Feela reluctantly put her coat back on after a long day at work and

went out the front door without telling her mother that she was leaving because she didn't feel like stopping to pick up something to eat.

In less than 30 minutes, Del'Feela was pulling up in front of Quail's apartment building about to park her car when he came walking up to the passenger door trying to hurry up and get in. "So, you had your bitch come and pick you up aye. Well good riddance because you're a fucking handful you good-for-only-fucking bastard," Quail's girlfriend said as Del'Feela drove away. Turns out, Quail was living with her.

Del'Feela looked over at Quail like what in the hell is going on, wanting an answer without asking the question. "Q who was that chick?" Del'Feela asked, driving down Goodfellow Avenue heading back home.

"That was this chick that was pushing up on me because I didn't want to renew my lease, so we could live together," Quail said, hoping that Del'Feela believed the lie he told. Quail got put out of his girlfriend's home because he wanted to come and go as he pleased and not pay any rent.

"Whatever you say Q. You have till Sunday to stay at my momma's house. Then you will have to vacate the premises," Del'Feela said as she pulled up to park in front of her mother's house.

Quail got out of Del'Feela's car and followed behind her as she walked inside her mother's house. *Shit, I haven't even thought about where this nigga is going to sleep because it ain't going to be with me every night until he leaves on Sunday*, Del'Feela thought.

Quail sat his trash bag full of clothes down on Del'Feela's bedroom floor to lay the law down in her mother's house. "Listen, we aren't having any sex unless I'm really up to giving you some, and I'll pay $30 a week," Quail said before plopping down on Del'Feela's bed and grabbing the remote to turn on her television.

Ain't that a bitch, Del'Feela thought.

C' That's Why I Don't Fool with Women

I Think I Got Shit Under Control

It had been almost a month since Quail had moved into Del'Feela's mother's house with the lady of the house not even knowing he was basically living there. Del'Feela was taking Quail back and forth to work like a parent taking a child to school. *This shit has to end or I'm going to go crazy*, Del'Feela thought as she watched Quail go into the check cashing place. It was Friday and Del'Feela missed hanging out with her girlfriends. She had to stay home when Quail was there, because he didn't have any place to go and she didn't want to leave him alone in the house.

"Here's yo money," Quail said, handing over $30 in cash.

0"…..Quail, you keep that money because you're going to need it for wherever you're staying tonight," Del'Feela said as she headed home so Quail could get his belongings and leave.

As soon as Del'Feela parked her car, Quail slapped her so hard that she saw stars. "I ain't going nowhere but inside of yo momma's house so that you can fix me something to eat," he said.

Del'Feela had to get her thoughts together right fast because she just could not believe that Quail did the unthinkable and had put his hands on her.

Sherre Still

"Quail, I'm going to go in the house and get yo motherfucking shit, so you can go on your way," she said as she got out of the car and headed to the front door.

Quail refused to leave and threatened to kick Del'Feela's ass. Del'Feela recorded the threats and called the police. Now what Quail had forgotten was that Del'Feela knew that he was on probation for assault. Del'Feela really didn't want to go to the extreme until Quail had put his hands on her, so she had no other choice but to call the police. Quail took off running away from Del'Feela's mother's house once he discovered Del'Feela was calling the police. Running like a track star trying to find the finish line, Quail left to keep from getting locked up. After the police arrived to get Del'Feela's report, she called her girlfriends to find out if anyone was available to go out for a drink, because she needed one.

C' That's Why I Don't Fool with Women

Adult Daycare Is Working Out Just Fine

Ree had to pat herself on the back as she headed to the adult daycare to pick her grandmother up after getting off from work. Ree's mother was unable to care for her mother so she let Ree make the decisions. As Ree walked in the beautiful, black-owned adult daycare, she was greeted by the owner, Ms. Shields. "Hello Ms. Shields. How did grandma do today?" Ree asked with a smile.

Ms. Shields laughed and asked Ree to follow her. Ree followed Ms. Shields and heard the piano playing, knowing it was her grandmother making music. Mary-Lee's wig swayed as she rocked her head from side to side playing *She Would Trust In The Lord*. Ree told Ms. Shields that her grandmother use to play lead piano in the church choir every Sunday until her health got so she just couldn't do it anymore. Mary-Lee smiled once she saw Ree's face.

"Y'all that's my granddaughter," Mary-Lee said as she got up from the piano to leave. Ree thanked the staff and Ms. Shields for taking such good care of her grandmother before signing her out for the day. Before they pulled off, Ree handed her grandmother an envelope.

Sherre Still

"Woo wee that's right! It's Friday! Payday," Mary-Lee said with a huge smile on her face as she counted the 51-dollar bills.

When Ree took her grandmother around Saint Louis looking at adult daycare centers, she accidently told her grandmother what the places were, upsetting her grandmother. After calming her down, Ree found a place she liked. "So, grandma you like working at the adult daycare?" Ree asked as she drove to the restaurant to pick up dinner for later.

"Yeah baby, the job is easy. I set the table every morning and help sweep the floor and tell people to sit their butt down in the wheelchair when they know damn well they can barely stand up. Here, take a couple of dollars and put it in your gas tank, because if it wasn't for you I wouldn't be making no extra money," Mary-Lee said. She handed Ree $10 that Ree refused to take.

Ree hoped and prayed that her grandmother's personality wouldn't change, because she seemed like her normal self since taking the antibiotics and being seen by the doctor for a follow-up.

C' That's Why I Don't Fool with Women

He Got a Lot of Nerve

Just as he had done before, Quail called Del'Feela to say he was sorry and ask for forgiveness. "Quail, where are you and why are you calling me of all people after you put your hands on me?" Del'Feela asked while she walked in the other room, not wanting her male friend who was over for a visit to hear.

"I'm calling you because we need each other. You are the coffee to my cream, and I'm the butter to your bread, baby. Please hear me out and don't hang up," Quail begged.

"I ain't nothing to you Quail. Where are you at?" she asked, still trying to find out where her abuser was located.

"I'm outside your front door. Please let me in," Quail said before the line went dead.

Del'Feela hurried up and called the police, hoping they would get there in time to lock Quail up. Quail had passed out from drinking too much. When the police arrived, they nudged him with the nightstick, trying to wake him up. Finally, after the third try, the police were able to place the handcuffs on Quail and tell him that he was under arrest. "I didn't do anything," he yelled.

Del'Feela went back to entertaining her male company once the police car drove away with Quail in it.

C' That's Why I Don't Fool with Women

He's Going to Do Some Jail Time for Putting His Hands On Me

Like working a 9 to 5, Del'Feela would go to the courthouse to check on evidence so that nothing would be left out. Satisfied that everything was taken care of after finding out the court date, Del'Feela got in her car so that she could do her regular errands and pick up her mother's medicine at the drug store before going home. Del'Feela answered her cellphone when she saw her friend was calling. "Did you get everything taken care of?" Zantaneek asked just to be nosey.
"Yes, girl I did. I turned over a recording of Quail threatening me and the letter that asshole mailed from jail stating that I was an informant for the police since his ass got locked up,".
"Well as a friend I say you need your girlfriends to help you pick a decent man to date because you don't know how to pick'em,".
Ain't that about a bitch. Well I know you like women and that you're dating my first cousin Pasadena, Del'Feela thought. "Girl bye! You couldn't pick a man for me to date if you tried," Del'Feela said laughing.

Sherre Still

I Had to Send His Ass Back Home to His Momma

Sharia was damn near getting on Ila's last nerves asking her how she took the steps to move on with her life without a husband. "I love him, but I can't let Wentzville keep disrespecting me," Sharia said out of anger.

This was really the first time that Ila had ever heard Wentzville had done something wrong. Yes, Ila knew that no marriage was perfect. It just seemed like Sharia and Wentzville had things all together all the time. After listening to Sharia talk for what seemed like two hours, Ila said she needed to get off the phone to take a nap before going to work later.

"Damn, Sharia is long-winded" Ila said rubbing her ear as she called Ree.

"What's up Mrs. Missing in Action since we came back from our vacation? How come I haven't heard from you or seen you at work?" Ila said, concerned about her friend.

Ree placed the plate of hot food before her grandmother to eat for dinner as she bowed her head when Mary-Lee prayed before eating. "Girl, a lot has been going on since we been back home. Falcon and I were talking about me breaking my lease and moving back home and then I went to visit my grandmother and found out she has a slight touch of dementia. So, in the

C' That's Why I Don't Fool with Women

meantime I have grandma staying with me here at the apartment and I've placed her in an adult daycare that she thinks she works at Monday through Friday," Ree said smiling at her grandmother as she said that dinner was sho nuff good.

"Damn Ree, that's a lot that has been going on in your world. I pray that things get better, because I truly know what you are going through. Let me catch you up on what's going on with my girlfriends that you know. Del'Feela's on and off again boyfriend that she helped get out of jail for time served from assaulting another woman about six or seven months ago is locked up for assaulting her. Zantaneek called and told me about it because she just couldn't keep the story to herself. Sharia put Wentzville out of the house for some reason and called me to ask how to do this and that on her own as though she is leaving her marriage," Ila said.

"What! I thought Sharia and her husband had things all together. I'm really sorry to hear that because I like Sharia and it's hard to be a single parent, especially with four children, but I'm not saying that it can't be done," Ree said. Ree and Ila talked a few minutes more before Ree had to get off of the phone to take care of her grandmother.

Sherre Still

Our Day in Court

Del'Feela represented herself since she was well-versed in law and didn't have funds to waste hiring a lawyer. Zantaneek came in the court room to sit in the back and see how things went for her friend. During the proceedings, the judge reviewed the incident and then went through the file of evidence that Del'Feela had provided.

"Ms. Wrangler, I'm sorry this has happened to you, and I will grant you the restraining order, but Mr. Stone will be released for time served," the judge said as Quail winked at Del'Feela and mouthed "bitch."

Del'Feela kept her composure as though things were all good because they certainly were. Quail stood to his feet beside his public defender, thanking him for doing a good job with thoughts of going to get him a cold beer once released to the Saint Louis streets. The judge signed the last document with Quail grinning from ear to ear.

"Mr. Stone, you will be turned over to county for violating your parole," the judge said as the officer placed Quail's hands behind his back and put the handcuffs on. Quail was in a state of shock because he didn't see that situation happening to him. Del'Feela winked at Quail and then mouthed "bye bitch" as

C' That's Why I Don't Fool with Women

the officer took him out of the court room. Zantaneek and Del'Feela laughed, giving each other five when they got on the elevator. They laughed about Quail thinking that he was going to be released to the streets.

Sherre Still

I Thought She Was Getting Better

After picking her grandmother up from adult daycare, Ree took her to the doctor because something just didn't seem right. Ree sat in the room exhausted, with her head in her hands. Turns out, her grandmother had a urinary tract infection and needed medication that came with side effects that Ree was familiar with. *God give me strength,* Ree thought. It seemed as if she was the only grandchild that Mary-Lee had to depend on because none of her cousins offered to assist.

When Ree got in the car, Falcon called to check on her, so she told him all about her grandmother's appointment. "Why don't you move back home and make it easier for yourself and let me help you take care of your loved one?" Falcon suggested.

This was one of the things Ree loved about her old man, but she just couldn't and wouldn't take him up on his offer until he did what she requested, which was tell his daughter Lovette to move out of the house.

"Fal, you know I told you I'm not coming back to the house until you do what you need to do to have our house in order," Ree said.

C' That's Why I Don't Fool with Women

"Ree, Lovette left the house yesterday mad because she thinks you're brainwashing me. She thinks I can't think for myself," Falcon said. Ree was pleased to know that Falcon had put Lovette out of her house, so she told her husband that in about a week she would return home.

"So, you don't live at home with your husband?" Mary-Lee asked her granddaughter.

Ree was caught so off guard by her grandmother's question, not thinking that she was even paying any attention. *Shit, it can't hurt me to tell grandma my personal business because she's not going to remember what I told her anyway,* Ree thought.

"No grandma I don't live with my husband now because we had some differences that now we are working on," she replied.

"Well if you ask me, I know you didn't ask me the question, but I say that you should go back home to your husband where you belong," Mary-Lee said, giving good family advice.

Grandma is going to be just fine. She's acting normal as usual once again, Ree thought as they both sat at the drug store and waited on the prescription to be filled.

Ree took her grandmother's advice and went home to her husband where she belonged. Falcon came out of the house when he saw Ree's BMW in the driveway.

"Thank you Fal for helping us in the house," Ree said.

"Ree, what are you thanking me for? Mary-Lee is family. I'm just glad that you have returned home to me so that we can really work things out," Falcon said.

Ree was glad she didn't make a hasty decision by going through with the divorce. As though she was in her apartment, Ree went to whip up something easy to cook for her grandmother and Falcon for dinner and then went to take a shower afterwards. Falcon ushered Mary-Lee upstairs. "You know what?" Mary-Lee said as she sat on the bed in the guest bedroom.

"What is it grandma?" Falcon asked, expecting to hear something funny because Mary-Lee was something else.

"You are a fine boy. You hear me child?" Mary-Lee said, just smiling at Falcon. Falcon thanked Mary-Lee for the compliment and then left the guest bedroom so that she could get dressed for bed.

Sherre Still

When Falcon walked into the bedroom, Ree was waiting for him. She was stressed out from working 12 hours every other day on top of taking care of her grandmother and needed Falcon to take some of that tension away. Falcon slowly took off his V-neck T-shirt and pajama pants then got in bed with his wife. They kissed and touched one another. "I really missed you being here every night with me," Falcon said as he moved down to the lower half of Ree's body.

Ree was lost for words as Falcon took control of pleasing her. *Damn, this feels so good. I really needed this tender loving care,* Ree thought as her husband gently turned her over and entered her from behind. After about twenty minutes of love making, both Falcon and Ree fell asleep.

They were sleeping like babies when they were awakened by screaming and yelling. Ree jumped out of bed trying to find her robe so she could go and check on her grandmother. She dashed out of the bedroom with Falcon following right behind her. Ree walked in the guest bedroom to see her grandmother standing in the nude holding a lamp in hand as though she was going to hit her granddaughter. "GET AWAY FROM ME SO I CAN GET OUT OF HERE AND GO HOME VIOLET," Mary-Lee screamed. Ree's heart sank because she knew that the dementia had gotten worse. Falcon walked out of the guest bedroom to call for the paramedics, so they could get Mary-Lee to the hospital right away.

"Grandma it's me, Ree, your granddaughter. Violet is your daughter and my mother. Let me help you get dressed so I can take you home grandma," Ree said, shedding tears because she barely could hold it together seeing her grandmother that way. Mary-Lee took a swing at Ree with the lamp as her granddaughter approached her.

The paramedics walked into the guest bedroom but Ree yelled "GET THE HELL OUT" because her grandmother wasn't decent. Finally, after Ree got her grandmother to put her pajamas back on, she allowed the paramedics to come in the room to assist her grandmother. Ree rode to the hospital in the ambulance after getting dressed quickly with Falcon saying that he would follow.

"Hey, Ree baby, where are we going?" Mary-Lee asked with a smile, being now so calm.

"We're going to the hospital to see the doctor," Ree said.

C' That's Why I Don't Fool with Women

"Ok baby," Mary-Lee said as she nodded off to sleep.

The doctor's performed several tests and discovered Mary-Lee had a reaction to the antibiotics she was prescribed for the urinary tract infection. Falcon suspected that was the case and assured his wife that everything was going to be just fine and not to worry. Mary-Lee was admitted into the hospital so Ree called her job to request time off from work. Falcon went home at Ree's request because she knew he had to be at work later that day.

Sherre Still

Discharged

It had been a horrible nine days while Ree's grandmother was in the hospital. Ree had only left her grandmother's bedside for a few hours to go home and change clothes, only to return and find that her grandmother had pulled her IV out or had fallen out of bed. Never once did Ree share with the staff that she was a registered nurse and had knowledge of their medical terminology when the interns made their rounds each day. "Can my grandmother have a sitter tonight, because I'm due to return to work," Ree said to the charge nurse who wasn't too fond of her.

"Ma'am we are short staffed, and our budget is too low to call and ask for a sitter to spend the night at your grandmother's bedside. You don't have a family member that can come and sit with your loved one?" the charge nurse asked with a smile.

Ree understood clearly that the charge nurse was being a real bitch in a white uniform. "Call your nurse administrator so I can have a chat with him or her instead since there's no need in talking to you," Ree said with a smile that said, "see bitch, you're not as smart as you may seem."

C' That's Why I Don't Fool with Women

Ree got exactly what she wanted. Once the sitter arrived to sit at Ree's grandmother's side, Ree left satisfied with plans to return bright and early when she got off from work since she was working the night shift. Nobody else had been by to see Mary-Lee.

After leaving the hospital, Ree drove to her apartment to pick up her mail since she hadn't been there since she had been living at home again. As she drove she thought about how upset her mom was that she didn't call her until two days after her grandmother had been admitted. Just then, her mother called her. *She must know I'm thinking about her*, Ree thought as she answered the phone.

"Hey, how is momma doing?" Violet asked, acting like she was concerned about her mother.

You would know if you would have fixed your mouth to ask me to pick you up or if you had thought about catching a cab to the hospital so that you could see how grandma is doing, Ree thought, wanting to speak her mind but knowing it was best to respect her parent.

"Grandma is doing just fine. Have you called Uncle Duck and Uncle Buck-Lu to let them know that their mother is in the hospital?" Ree asked since her mother was asking questions.

"I'm glad to hear momma is doing ok, and yes I called my brothers. I have to go. I'll talk to you later," Violet said, cutting the conversation short.

Damn that was odd, Ree thought. She had love for her mother, but they weren't the best of friends. Ree exited the elevator and ran into Larissa, the building manager. She had just finished showing an apartment down the hall from Ree's place. "Hey Larissa, I didn't know that apartment down the hall was vacant," Ree said while unlocking her door.

Larissa analyzed Ree's style in dress, admiring the Gucci jogging suit and tennis shoes along with the large leather hobo bag. Ree was about to walk into her apartment when she realized that Larissa was getting ready to come in behind her. Ree turned around with a smile but was ready to kick some ass if Larissa was on some stupid acting stuff. "Girl, I wanted to come in and talk to you to find out why you are moving out," Larissa said.

This bitch is crazy to be asking me my personal business, Ree thought. As a person who paid her rent on time and wasn't a nuisance to the property, Ree wasn't giving any explanation.

"It's good seeing you, Larissa, but I have to go," Ree said as she walked into her apartment. Walking through her apartment, Ree frowned at the smell of trash coming from the kitchen. Ree spent an hour cleaning up the apartment and packing her clothes before calling Falcon to let him know she was heading home.

Del'Feela wasn't feeling well and had a bad cough that she just couldn't get rid of after trying to nurse it herself, so she called Ila to see if she had any suggestions since she was a nurse. She told Ila she had been coughing like that for about two months and now had an odd discharge, so Ila suggested she see her gynecologist immediately.

After talking to Del'Feela, Ila called Ree. Falcon was rubbing Ree's feet when the phone rang. "Let me tell you about that hoe of Saint Louis," Ila said. "Del'Feela called me talking about she is coughing bad and can't get rid of it and she has a discharge coming out of her body. What female tells someone that and doesn't make an appointment to see a doctor? Huh?" Ila asked.

Ree was laughing at Falcon because he was licking her toes trying to arouse her and it was working. "Ila, can I call you back?" Ree asked.

"Where are you at?" Ila asked because she could hear a male voice in the background.

"I'm at home with Falcon, and he's messing with me. Let me get off this phone, because I have to work tonight," Ree said before hanging up.

So, Ree is back with her old man and didn't even tell me. I had to ask. Ain't that a bitch, Ila thought.

C' That's Why I Don't Fool with Women

The Next Morning

Ree knew very well that she should have just gone straight home to Falcon and gone to sleep after leaving her grandmother at the hospital. The twelve-hour night shift whooped Ree's ass because she had stayed awake practically till it was time for her to go to work. *Where in the hell is the nurse that's following me?* Ree wondered as she sat in the break room with the charge nurse looking at the clock. It was 8:15 and time for Ree to clock out. Finally, Blondie, the nurse following Ree, walked in the break room like she was in such a fucking rush. "Sorry that I was running a little late. I just got back from vacation and came to work straight from the airport," Blondie said as she threw her belongings in her locker.

No one cares about where you just came from. The point is you're late, bitch, Ree thought as she sat at the table ready to give the report as though she was rapping to the beat in her head to get the fuck out of dodge and go home. Blondie sat across from Ree as she gave the report, asking a million dumb ass questions that really didn't pertain to any of the patients she was going to be taking care of. Ree hurried up and got her purse before anyone could say anything to her so that she could clock out and go home. As soon as Ree got in the car her cellphone rang. It was the hospital her grandmother was in.

"Hello" Ree answered, barely having energy to talk.

"Good morning is this Ms. Mary-Lee's granddaughter Ree that I'm speaking with?" the person asked.

"Yes, this is Mary-Lee's granddaughter you're speaking with. What can I do for you?" Ree asked, hoping she wasn't getting a call that her grandmother had yet another fall.

"My name is Runner. I'm one of the day charge nurses. I was calling to let you know that your grandmother will be getting discharged today. Now the social worker states that your grandmother has a senior citizen apartment. Will she be going back there to live alone?" the nurse asked.

Ree told the nurse that her grandmother will be living with her and in adult daycare during the day while she was at work. Because she worked in the medical profession, Ree knew that the nurse and the social worker were trying to place her grandmother in a nursing home since she had Medicaid and they thought she didn't have anyone capable to take care of her.

"I'll be at the hospital around 1:00 to pick my grandmother up," Ree said before hanging up the phone as she pulled into her garage happy that she made it home safely.

Ree took her clog nursing shoes off, left them in the garage and rushed upstairs. "Well good morning stepmother. I can smell that you have fucked your way back into the house," Lovette said as she left the house with the last of her belongings.

"Yes, I did step-daughter. Hopefully you can take notes and find you a man and do the same to get a permanent residence," Ree said, shutting the front door and then changing the security code so that unwanted guests wouldn't be allowed to get in.

Noon came so fast that Ree dreaded getting out of bed to go get her grandmother, but she knew that she had to go. By 12:40 p.m. Ree was walking down the hallway of the hospital prepared to take her grandmother home with her until the social worker stopped her from walking into the room.

"Hello Ree, can we talk privately in the room down the hallway?" the social worker asked.

"Sure," Ree said, following the social worker so they could talk.

C' That's Why I Don't Fool with Women

Ree was hoping that nothing was majorly wrong with her grandmother, but then she figured if it was then it wouldn't have been the social worker talking to her. It would be the nurse giving that kind of information.

"Ree, I asked to talk to you privately so that there won't be a scene out in the hallway. Your mother Violet called the hospital and said she and her brother will be coming to pick your grandmother up because you don't have power of attorney. I didn't want to talk in front of your grandmother about this matter and get her all upset," the social worker said, looking at the door to make sure the security guard was standing nearby. Word spread that Ms. Mary-Lee's granddaughter was a bitch after Ree demanded a sitter.

Ree was totally caught off guard with what the social worker said. She just didn't want to believe that her mother would stoop so low. *I've been doing more than my share as a granddaughter to take care of grandma when she and any other family member could have been doing their share,* Ree thought mad as hell. With knowing what it took to take care of someone with her grandmother's disease, Ree knew her mother wasn't going to be able to take care of her since she was somewhat sick herself.

Still pissed off, Ree sat outside of the hospital looking at the front entrance to see if her mother and uncle would actually show up. Within 15 minutes, Ree saw her mother and Uncle Buck-Lu walking into the hospital together. *This is crazy,* Ree thought. She felt like it was a dream as she drove home crying her eyes out.

Del'Feela got dressed after being examined by the doctor and tried not to think the worst. *I can't be pregnant because I just took a pregnancy test day before yesterday. Please don't let me have a STD or I'm going to be celibate for the rest of my life. I'm going to have to use sex toys to please myself.* The doctor walked in the room to give her the results.

"Well young lady, it looks like you have a horrible bacterial infection," the doctor said as he wrote in her chart. Relieved that she had something treatable, Del'Feela asked her doctor to call in her prescription so that it would be ready when she went to pick it up.

"Thank you doctor. You're the best," Del'Feela said. She was dressed like an old lady, so her doctor wouldn't think bad of her if she had a disease.

Sherre Still

"You're welcome. Just make sure the person that you're having oral sex with has a clean mouth next time," the doctor said before leaving out of the room to see his next patient.

Del'Feela had to think hard. Then it came to her. "That fuck'ca Pronto with the bad breath who is a manager at the movie theater probably gave me this infection," Del'Feela said, wanting to drive to his place of employment and tell him to clean his mouth. He was the only one she allowed to orally please her due to him having a small one.

By the time Ree got back home, Falcon was there waiting on her, so he could help take care of her grandmother. "Hey babe! Where is queen Mary-Lee?" Falcon asked with a smile.

Ree began to cry as she told him what happened.

"Ree, calm down and get yourself together. Then call your mother and ask her what's going on. It must be a reason why that happened," Falcon said as he hugged his wife and gently rubbed her back.

After getting herself together, Ree sat down, dialed her mother's telephone number and patiently waited for her to answer the phone.

"Hello," Violet answered.

"Hey momma, why did you tell the social worker that grandma will be staying with you when you and her don't get along and you're sick yourself?" Ree asked.

"Listen Ree, this is my momma not yours. You wouldn't even take me in when I had surgery, but you took my momma in to live with you. Buck-Lu and I got taking care of our momma under control," Violet said with an attitude.

"Now this is the mother I do remember when I lived at home and had to bare and grin it until I was able to take care of myself. Why did you or Uncle Buck-Lu tell the social worker that I was spending grandma's social security check as my own trying to make me look like a thief? I pulled out my work I.D. badge to let them know that I was a nurse and didn't need to take a dime of grandma's $762 for anything. And as far as you putting me in my place about not bringing you into my home to take care of you — momma you can't say that I didn't come over every other day to see about your needs, and I'm not the only child that you have. Good luck with taking care of grandma," Ree

C' That's Why I Don't Fool with Women

said. She hung up before she said something that she would never be able to take back.

So, this is what it's all about. Momma felt that I love grandma more than her. So, to get back at me she takes grandma to live with her, trying to look like the Good Samaritan daughter to the rest of the family members that don't give a good got damn, Ree thought.

When Ila got some free time, she called Del'Feela to find out about her visit to the doctor. "Girl I have a bad bacterial infection, and the doctor suggested that I make sure whoever I'm having oral sex with has a clean mouth," Del'Feela said laughing.

Ila had to look at the phone. *This bitch is crazy*, she thought.

"Bye, Del'Feela. Get you some rest," Ila said before hanging up the phone.

C that's why I don't fool with women, because once they find out all of your personal business they hang up, Del'Feela thought before going to sleep.

Coming Soon

Business, Life and Copyrights

We're not talking the cut-throat music business where an artist works for years making pennies on the damn dollar. We're not talking about a worn-out musician who is ready to retire. This is all about the book business where your work can stole in seconds electronically. With just a few keystrokes, your work can be snatched and suddenly you find you're not going to make a dime for your hard work because no one ever knew that it was yours.

Jewel is a 40-something wife and mother that aspires to be a published author. All she set out to do was leave something behind that would make her children proud. Jewel's plans are thwarted when she meets two entrepreneur scammers who use their exceptional talents to gain her trust, steals her work and present it as their own. After years of stealing people's work, hell catches up with the scammers when Jewel uncovers their bullshit games. This book is dedicated to aspiring authors.

On a warm, sunny day, Jewel drove her 2017 Mustang convertible with the top down on St. Charles Rock Road. She was just counting the motherfucking days down to retirement from the health care business. *Woo, I can't wait until my last damn day of work. You talking about sleeping all morning long and not worrying about being on time for work. That's what the fuck I can't wait for,* Jewel thought as she walked into the print shop to pick up an order. Jewel stood before the customer counter at 5'11 wearing a black business suit. She had brown skin, brown eyes and shoulder-length hair. The gentleman spotted Jewel walking toward the building and recognized her right away. He put her order in the bag so that she wouldn't have to wait.

"Good morning Ms. Boss Lady," he said, giving her a friendly smile.

"Good morning Graphic! How are you doing this beautiful morning?" she asked, returning the friendly smile.

"I'm doing just fine, Ms. Boss Lady. I saw you getting out of your car, so I rushed to bag your order. I didn't want you to have to wait. Your total is $109.56. I put a 50 percent off coupon in the bag for your next," he said.

Jewel fumbled through her purse to find her wallet so that she could pay. She pulled out her credit card and handed it to Graphic. He completed the transaction and tossed the receipt in the bag.

"Thank you Graphic; you are so helpful. If you don't mind me asking, how long have you been working here at the print shop?" she asked.

"I'll say around maybe three or four months, but I'm just helping a friend out until he gets the right crew of employees to operate his business. Then I'm going to go back to what I do best," he said.

Jewel gave Graphic a curious look. "Look around the print shop, Ms. Boss Lady. When a church has a special event, or an entertainer comes to town or a corporation needs advertisements, I'm the man to get the job done. I like working for myself. It's less stressful, and I don't have to work when I don't want to."

Jewel looked around the print shop at the posters Graphic had designed for an upcoming play coming to the Pox's Theater. "Wow! You have been blessed with so much talent. I love your work. It looks like art," she said

"Thanks for the compliment, Ms. Boss Lady. I'm not trying to brag, but I also just finished publishing my own book and designing it myself. Take a look at it," Graphic said, sticking his chest out to impress Jewel.

Jewel admired the well-designed cover and opened the book to read an excerpt. She was very impressed to learn that Graphic had written, designed and published his book. Being a published author was one of Jewel's long-time dreams. She didn't want to do it for the fame and wealth. She just wanted to leave a body of work behind that her family would be proud of.

Looking at her watch, Jewel noticed that she needed to be going. She didn't want to hear her cousin complain about her being two minutes late for work.

"Well Graphic I need to be getting out of here. I don't want to be late for work. It was so good talking to you. I'll see you around soon," she said before leaving the print shop. Graphic waved goodbye as he walked back over to his desk to fulfill someone's design work order.

While driving to work, Jewel couldn't stop thinking about the conversation that she had with Graphic. She couldn't get over the fact that he had published his own book. She reflected on how professional the cover looked. The excerpt she read flowed perfectly. Jewel had started writing books five years ago as a hobby. When relatives visited Jewel, they insisted that she share her stories with the world.

She turned down the music as she pulled up in the parking lot to prepare her mind to deal with a day at work with her cousin. As soon as Jewel walked in the private duty agency, her cousin was ready to bitch because payroll hours hadn't been turned in to the company that did the payroll.

"Where in the hell have you been, Jewel? Don't you realize that you're late for work?" Roxanne asked pissed off.

"I was picking up your shit for your motherfucking business, Roxanne. Here are your brochures for the job fair that you forgot all about. You can thank me later and try to start appreciating when someone is trying to have your back. There's not one employee here in the office, and you're bitching that I'm late," Jewel said as she stormed past Roxanne.

Jewel thought about retiring and wondered what Roxanne would do. After all, everyone thought Jewel was the person in charge. She put on some jazz music, turned on her computer and began doing Roxanne's job by forwarding the hours that the employees worked so everyone would get paid on time. Roxanne barged into Jewel's office with a stack of papers and dropped them on her desk. "Cuz, would you please file these papers that my secretary hadn't gotten around to yet?" Roxanne asked with a friendly smile, hoping that Jewel would take on the additional task.

Jewel just gave Roxanne a look. She didn't have to say a word to let Roxanne know she wanted to be left alone.

"Thank you, my Jewel. I don't know what I'm going to do without you once you retire, because I haven't even been interviewing anyone for your position," Roxanne admitted before going back to her office like she really had something to do. As Jewel worked on the payroll, the telephone rang, breaking her concentration. It was Jewel's husband Lotrel.

"Hey baby! I just called to say have a good day and to let you know that things are going to be alright," he said, trying to make things right between them after an argument earlier that morning.

Jewel smiled when she heard her husband apologizing for upsetting her.

"I'm sorry too for saying what I said, Lotrel. You know I love you,"

"Well, let me get going to work since the kids are all gone off to school. I'll have dinner for you when you get home. Remember baby, have a good day, and I love you too," Lotrel said before hanging up the telephone.

Jewel and Lotrel were college sweethearts with four beautiful children. With a huge smile on her face, Jewel went back to doing payroll so that Roxanne wouldn't come in her office with another duty for her to get started on before lunch.

As Jewel tried to finish the payroll, Mrs. Bones, Roxanne's secretary that needed to retire along with Jewel, walked in. Looking at the stack of papers on Jewel's desk, Mrs. Bones realized that her boss had asked her family member to do what she was going to get around to doing sooner or a later.

"Morning Jewel! I see your cousin has asked you to do additional work for the day. Here's a good hot cup of coffee that I brought for you my dear. I'm not talking about your cousin, but I'm just going to tell you how I feel about her. Ok?"

Mrs. Bones didn't wait for a response from Jewel before she continued. "Roxanne wants you to do this then she wants you to do that, so that's why I stick to doing the normal duties before going to the extra stuff that your cousin wants done. Well, let little ole me get back to work before I'm told to clock out and go home because I ain't doing nothing," Mrs. Bones said. She kept talking as she walked back to her desk.

Jewel laughed to herself because there wasn't anything little about Mrs. Bones. She weighed every bit of 310 pounds. Mrs. Bones wasn't only Roxanne's secretary. She was her mother-in-law too and knew everything about her son's personal life with her daughter-in-law.

The work day was going by so fast that Jewel finished everything that she needed to get done and couldn't wait to get off from work and go home to her family. As usual, Jewel was the last person to leave the office, so she locked up for the evening like normal. She set the security alarm, locked the door and walked to her car with the thought of seeing her family. Jewel was about to stop and pick up some food for dinner until she remembered that her husband promised to take care of dinner for the night.

When Jewel pulled up in the driveway, she was greeted by her daughter, Bowleeta, who was washing dishes and saw Jewel through the kitchen window.

"Hey momma! How was your day work?" Bowleeta asked, happy to see her mother.

"I'm worn out, Bow. Your cousin Roxanne did nothing as usual today. She's going to miss me when I retire,"

"Well, let Roxanne figure that out when the time comes. She's been spoiled all of her life and used to having things her way. I'm surprised that you've been working for Roxanne as long as you have. Daddy bought dinner, so all you have to do is get comfortable and meet us at the dining room table,"

Jewel and Bowleeta walked inside of the house as the rest of the family came walking in the kitchen to greet their mother. Kirtland and Clifton walked over to their mother and gave her a hug. They were happy that she had come home earlier than normal to eat dinner with the family for once. Epiphany, the youngest of the Turner children, was in the dining room helping her father set the table for dinner.

"Hey momma," Epiphany yelled from the dining room.

"I know you better come in here and address your mother better than that little girl," Jewel said while taking off her sweater.

Epiphany walked into the kitchen to speak to her mother properly and give her a hug. After speaking to their mother, they all went their separate ways in the house until it was time to eat dinner. Lotrel walked up behind Jewel as she was about to walk upstairs to change clothes. His strong, masculine hands rubbed her backside.

"You're not going to greet daddy with a kiss?" he asked with a devilish look on his face. Jewel turned around to give her husband some tongue. The kiss was long enough to get the physical fire burning between them.

"Let's call the kids down for dinner while we go upstairs for a quickie. It's been a long time, Jewel, and if you're a believer of God you know it ain't right to hold back loving from your husband,"

Jewel looked at her husband's erection showing through his jogging pants with thoughts of going along with his plans, because it *had* been a while since they had been sexually active. She had put Lotrel on sex punishment for wanting to hang out with his homeboys all of the time and neglecting their date nights. *Shit, I want to suck Lotrel's dick right now, but if the kids catch their momma on her knees sucking their daddy's dick in the kitchen, I won't be able to explain that,* Jewel thought.

"Baby, let's eat as a family since we are all here together. I promise to suck your dick and give you some pussy for dessert," Jewel said, winking at her husband while walking upstairs. She eased her dress pants down, showing Lotrel the crack of her ass.

Big boy calm down, Lotrel thought as he stood alone in the kitchen massaging his groin and thinking of his wife.

Dinner Time

Everyone bowed their heads to pray before eating dinner. "Amen," the Turner family said before passing the food around at the table. Lotrel had picked up two 12-piece chicken dinners with mashed potatoes and gravy, green beans, dinner rolls and apple pie. As they enjoyed dinner, they talked about school and sports activities. Clifton, 18, was a freshman at the community college. Kirtland, 15, was a sophomore in high school and a track star. Jewel and Lotrel had to keep reminding him to stay away from the girls and get his education, Bowleeta, 14, was a freshman in high school and just barely getting by. Epiphany, 13, was the baby girl of the family and an eighth-grade honor roll student. Lotrel was glad that he went with his instinct and purchased so much food. There was very little leftover for the next day.

After dinner, the children cleaned up the kitchen and Lotrel and Jewel turned in for the night. While Jewel showered, Lotrel set a romantic mood in the bedroom with candles and romantic music. It had been three weeks since Jewel had given him some loving. He laid on the bed and massaged his groin while he waited for Jewel to take care of his sexual needs. Jewel walked out of the bathroom in a body towel. "Is the bedroom door locked?" she asked, not wanting any interruption once they got started.

"Baby, come over here and get in bed. Now you know I locked the door so none of the nosey teens can come in here and crash our sex party," Lotrel said.

Jewel danced over to the bed as Lotrel smiled at her. "Yeah, do that dance baby. You looking sexy as shit. I miss being inside of you," he said.

The smell of Jewel's perfume took Lotrel to an ultimate high as she got closer to him. "Don't you think I know that?" she asked as she kissed him.

She straddled her husband in the middle of the bed as he gripped her ass cheeks tight just the way Jewel liked it. Jewel rotated her lower body in circular motion and squeezed her vaginal muscles tightly as she curved around her husband's manhood. "Damn, I love the hell out of you, Jewel," Lotrel said.

The Weekend

It was Saturday morning and Jewel was happy to have a day off. For once, she didn't have to listen to all of Roxanne's requests. Also, it was beauty shop day with her daughters. She looked forward to spending some quality time with them and finding out what was going on in their lives. Jewel rolled over in bed to see Lotrel still sleeping like a baby. *I put it down on my poor baby,* Jewel thought as she kissed her husband's forehead before getting out of bed to start her day. Bowleeta knocked on the bedroom door.

"Momma good morning. What time is our hair appointment?" she asked while brushing her teeth.

"Our appointment is at 9:00. I'm getting ready to take a shower, so tell your sister to get up and get ready," Jewel said as she headed to the bathroom.

"Epiphany! Momma said get your butt up or she's going to leave you behind if you're not ready when she gets dressed to go," Bowleeta yelled on her way back to her bedroom. Kirtland and Clifton were in their bedroom playing video games. They were happy that it wasn't a weekday. They finally got some time off from the hustle and bustle of school to chill.

After getting dressed, Jewel cooked breakfast. She didn't want to waste money buying breakfast when she could spend that money on something else.

She ate and then rushed to finish getting ready. "Lotrel, have you seen my car keys anywhere?" Jewel asked in hurry. She didn't want to be late for her hair appointment.

Clifton walked into the kitchen with Jewel's keys in hand. "Here you go, momma. Your keys were in the hallway upstairs. Why don't you just get an extra set of keys made so that you won't have to be looking for them at the last minute?" he asked.

Jewel didn't respond to her son's question. She just thanked him for finding her keys and walked out of the door.

"Momma, can I get the two strand twists?" Bowleeta asked while sitting in the backseat and applying her lip gloss.

"I thought you said you were getting micro braids like your sister and I are getting," Jewel said as she drove to the beauty shop praying it wasn't crowded as usual.

"I changed my mind. I don't want to be sitting in the chair all day, even though Zoputa will have two people braiding my hair," Bowleeta said while snapping her fingers to the music on the radio. Epiphany was in the passenger seat and looked at her mother like they were girlfriends having a conversation.

"Momma, now you know Bowleeta is always the confused one. Why do you even waste your time talking to her when she don't know what she wants?" Epiphany asked.

Jewel just laughed at her baby girl sounding like a comedian. While Epiphany kept running her mouth, Jewel drove around the crowded parking lot of the beauty salon until she finally found a spot. They all hoped that it wouldn't be a long wait before they started to get their hair braided. Jewel couldn't believe she let her daughters talk her into getting her hair braided along with them.

"Hey sista can I help you?" Zoputa asked as Jewel and her daughters walked into the beauty shop.

"Yes, my name is Jewel. We have a 9:00 appointment," Jewel said.

"Yes, yes, yes, I remember you, Jewel," Zoputa said, even though she really didn't remember setting the appointment.

Zoputa spoke her native African language to two of the ladies working in the shop as they put on fake smiles to greet Jewel and her daughters. "Ms. Jewel how do you expect to pay today?" Zoputa asked.

Jewel was caught a little bit off guard by the question, because she normally got her hair done first and paid later. "I was intending to pay by charge card," Jewel said, hoping she wasn't going to ruin her girl's day out by cussing the owner of the braiding shop out for asking a financial question in front of the other customers.

Jewel's daughters were already in the chairs, and Zoputa looked over at the ladies who worked for her. The ladies knew that look. It meant for them not to touch the girls' hair until she said so. Epiphany and Bowleeta were looking at their mother, hoping she wasn't going to cuss out the owner of the shop. They both wanted to get their hair braided and knew their mom would go off at any minute when rubbed the wrong way.

"I don't accept plastic, but if you're able to use an ATM card I have a machine in the back room here," Zoputa said as she pointed to the room behind her.

Ain't this a bitch! This hoe got at least 20 people braiding hair in this shop, and she has the audacity to tell me that she doesn't except credit card payments, Jewel thought. She was seconds away from telling that bitch to kiss her American black ass and telling her daughters to get in the car, so they could go someplace else to get their hair done. Jewel gave her daughters the eye.

"Momma please can we get our hair done here? You can keep my allowance for the month. Momma please," Bowletea begged with pleading eyes.

Jewel was still seconds away from saying, "We about to get the fuck out of here," but deep down inside she wanted to see how she would look with braids. She put her pride all the way to the side and decided to stick with the plan.

"Where is the ATM machine, and how much will it cost for the three of us to get our hair done? Two of us are getting micro braids and my oldest daughter wants two strand twists," Jewel said.

"Did you bring your own hair?" Zoputa asked.

"No, we didn't bring any hair with us," Jewel said. She didn't know she could bring her own hair because her daughters didn't mention it.

"I can sell you the hair since you didn't bring any with you. Micro braids with the human hair will be $250 each and the two strand twists with the synthetic hair will be $200," Zoputa said with an African accent.

Jewel calculated quickly in her head. The total was $700. She didn't expect to spend that much money in one day. She looked at Epiphany and Bowleeta, who were both staring at her with pleading eyes. Jewel asked again where the ATM was, so she could withdraw $700 to pay the braiders. After Jewel withdrew the money from the ATM, she put it in her wallet and walked back to the braiding area.

"Excuse me sista, but can you pay now?" Zoputa asked with a friendly smile.

Jewel was now pissed the fuck off, because there was no way she was going to pay someone $700 cash before everyone's hair was completely done.

"No, I can't pay now. I'll pay once our hair is completely done," Jewel said, returning the friendly smile and sitting in the styling chair next to her daughters.

Bowleeta and Epiphany looked at each other laughing because they knew their mother wasn't going to pay until they got their hair done. Zoputa spoke in her native language to five of the ladies that worked for her. They huffed and puffed as they spoke, but Jewel didn't care what the hell the women were talking about just as long as they didn't speak any English and disrespect her.

Zoputa wanted to get paid as soon as possible so she made sure two ladies worked on each of them. She went to the storage room where all the braiding hair was stored to get a few bags of human hair for Jewel to choose from. Jewel chose the 1B, 10-inch wet and wavy braiding hair because she didn't care for really long hair. She was happy to know that two braiders had been assigned, because she didn't want to be in the beauty shop all day and damn near night to get her hair done. For entertainment, Zoputa had Nigerian music playing as she sang and braided someone's hair.

When a man came into the shop, Jewel wondered why he was there. "I need to pay my cell phone bill," he said.

"I'll meet you over at the counter in just a minute," Zoputa said.

As Jewel watched the transaction, it dawned on her that the shop wasn't licensed. She and her daughters were in a bootleg braiding chop shop. *Un-*

fucking believable. There is no way this business could be operating in any of the fancy areas in St. Louis such as Clayton, La Due, Chesterfield, Webster or Rock Hill, Jewel thought.

Zoputa accepted the man's payment and then tried to sell him a new phone, insisting that he needed an upgrade.

"Naw, I'm good with the phone I got. I'll check you out when it's time to pay my bill next month," the man said before leaving the store with his friend. Instead of going back to her other customer to finish the braids, Zoputa went to the kitchen to heat up some food. She came back to the braiding area with a plate. *What the hell is she eating?* Jewel thought.

"Hey Zoputa, you gon' like that. I made it last night. It is pig ears, broiled catfish and broiled chicken to put on top of that rice," Nufaye said with a smile.

Zoputa added some lemon juice to the dish and sat on the stool behind her customer to eat the awful smelling food. Jewel thought she was going throw up as she smelled the food and watched Zoputa eat that mess.

A cab pulled up in front of the shop and a midget of a man walked in the braid chop shop and greeted Zoputa with a kiss on the cheek. "Have I had many customers this morning buying cell phones or making payments?" Igbo asked.

"Yes, yes, the people have been coming in making payments, and I sold four phones," Zoputa said.

So, this midget is Zoputa's husband, and he's a cabdriver too, Jewel thought as she looked at his wrinkled uniform and watched as he walked over to the cash register. Zoputa wiped her hands on her clothes and went back to braiding the woman's hair. Jewel was mad as hell that the customer didn't cuss Zoputa out for being so disrespectful. Within five minutes, the women braiding Epiphany's hair went to the back area and came back with their lunch. Jewel stopped the ladies from braiding her hair to stand up to speak loudly to Zoputa.

"Excuse me, Zoputa! Will there be a 50 percent discount for me and my daughters since you all take these silent lunch breaks without telling anyone what the hell is going on up in here?" Jewel asked.

The other customers pulled out their phones to record Jewel. Immediately, the two women who were braiding Epiphany's hair went to the kitchen to put away their food and went back to braiding Jewel's daughter hair.

"Did y'all wash y'all's hands before touching my baby's hair, because I don't want to leave smelling like that food y'all eating," Jewel said pissed off.

Zoputa spoke in her language to the ladies who were braiding Epiphany's hair. They frowned and poked their lips out, upset that Jewel had demanded their respect. It took only four hours for Bowleeta to get the two strand twists. Bowleeta looked at herself in the mirror and smiled. She couldn't wait to show off her new hairstyle at school on Monday.

"Your hair looks cute Bow," Epiphany said. Jewel gave Bowleeta thumbs up. Oke, one of Zoputa's friends, walked into the braid chop shop after getting off from work at the casino hotel. She wanted to find out if Zoputa needed her in the shop to braid hair. She was up for making a few extra dollars before heading home.

"Hey Oke! I'm very glad you stopped by the shop. As you see I need your help. Can you help Afafa out because she has a person coming in at 4:00," Zoputa said.

Oke nodded, greeted Afafa and got to work. "I see you keeping that full-time job still," Afafa said with a laugh.

"Yes, me will always keep a full-time job with health benefits. I'll work nights at the casino and days here if you all need me to help out to make the cash money," Oke said, bragging that she was a hustler.

These Africans have taken the money-making game to another level, Jewel thought. She couldn't believe all of the businesses they were running. Zoputa's business cell phone rang. She pulled the phone out of her bra to answer it.

"Braid, Twist and Cornrow," Zoputa said. After pausing to allow the customer to speak, she replied.

"If you want to come in, today is fine. Business is very slow. Yes, yes, I'll be here waiting till you get off from work at 7," Zoputa said. Once she finished the call, she put the phone back in her bra. Business wasn't slow at all that day. There were 20 styling chairs in the cell phone/unlicensed braid shop with customers sitting in every chair. Jewel began to tally up how much money was being made. Five customers were getting micro braids and paying

$250 each. Four people were getting two strand twists at $200 each. Five people getting goddess cornrows at $110 each. Six people were getting boxes braids at $230 each. That was $3,980 tax-free and the day wasn't over. *I can't make that being a nurse. I'm in the wrong damn profession now that I'm scoping their master plan out,* Jewel thought.

The customer sitting next to Jewel wasn't pleased with her hairstyle at all. She had all kinds of complaints. Zoputa looked at the woman who did the customer's hair. "We gotta get this money," Zoputa whispered.

"You asked for this hairstyle. What is it that you don't like about your hair?" Zoputa asked the unhappy customer.

"This style makes my head look so big," the woman said while frowning up in the mirror.

Zoputa just listened to her complain for another five minutes before saying something.

"Listen, next time you come when you can afford to buy the human hair. I'll give you a good price. Ok?" Zoputa said. She wanted to get paid and get rid of the unhappy customer as soon as possible.

The woman sat back in the styling chair as though she was going to get her hair redone.

Zoputa walked over to the unhappy customer, barely picking her big, fat, plump feet up off of the floor. She was dragging her flip flops across the floor as she walked.

"The cost for your hair is $150," Zoputa insisted.

The unhappy customer paid the amount Zoputa said that she owed for getting her hair done with the promise that she would never be coming back there again to get her hair done. Zoputa didn't care if the customer ever came back as long as she paid that day.

After putting the cash in her pocket, Zoputa greeted a walk-in customer and listened to her request. Zoputa looked around the shop, thinking she would have plenty of money to wire back home to Nigeria where her mother still lived. The American dollar was triple in value in Nigeria so Zoputa's mother and three sisters and their children could live like queens. An old Nigerian woman, Zoputa's mother-in-law, walked in and hugged Zoputa.

"Hey, momma," Zoputa said as she smiled and hugged her mother-in- law, Dilola.

"Business is looking good I see," Dilola said as she looked around at all of the customers getting their hair braided. "I had a good day. I've finally been approved for food stamps, and I moved into my new senior citizen apartment yesterday. You should stop by to see it if you ever get off from work."

Zoputa just smiled. Dilola put away her purse in one of the storage cabinets and walked over to assist one of the braiders. Jewel sat there and thought about writing a book called *Unlicensed Africans Braiding Hair and Getting Mother Fucking Paid*. Jewel felt like it was an insult to even be in that place getting her hair done after connecting so many dots right in her face, because she had a grandmother and aunt who owned a beauty salon. Growing up, Jewel saw how hard running a business was for them. Paying taxes, rent, insurance and business license fees and having the board of health make surprise visits at their beauty salon was hard. They dealt with customers who left happy saying they loved their hair styles and then came back four days later to complain. That's why Jewel never wanted to become a beautician. The Nigerians are taught as children how to braid hair. By the time they are adults, they have mastered the craft, so they come to the U.S. without going to cosmetology school to get licensed.

Finally, Epiphany and Jewel were finished, and they were pleased with their hair. Jewel was determined not to pay if she didn't like her hair. Reluctantly, Jewel paid cash for her and her daughters' hair.

"Thank you! Come again," Zoputa said.

Jewel put on some lipstick to enhance her beauty as her daughters complimented her on her hair. When they got in the car, Bowleeta asked her mother if they were still going to get their nails done. Jewel told her daughters that they were going home after paying that much money for their hair.

"Momma, does you head hurt from your hair being braided?" Epiphany asked.

"Actually, my head doesn't hurt at all. If it did I would have had to ask the ladies who were braiding my hair to take it back down. You know your momma don't like pain baby," Jewel said as she drove home.

Bowleeta and Epiphany got out of the car right away once their mother turned off the engine to run in the house to show off their new hairstyles. Clifton and Kirtland were playing video games on the flat screen television in the living room that their mother told them not to play on.

"How do you like our hair big-head boys?" Bowleeta asked her brothers as she and Epiphany posed in front of the television.

"Get the fuck out of our way," Clifton said as his mother walked in the front door.

Jewel knew her ears and eyes were playing tricks on her when she heard Clifton use profanity and saw her sons in her living room playing video games. She slammed the front door to let Clifton know she heard him. Jewel stood in front of both of her sons with her daughters moving out of the way.

"You better unhook the damn game from my television, and Clifton if I ever hear you using profanity again in this house you're going to be sorry. Do you understand me?" Jewel asked.

Kirtland had already started unhooking the video game from the living room television because he knew his mother was going to demand it. He quietly walked out of the living room, praying that he wouldn't get cussed out or put on punishment for disobeying his mother. Jewel walked in the kitchen to wash her hands and look in the refrigerator to see what she could throw together for dinner.

"Chicken salad and garlic cheese bread will be dinner tonight," she said to herself as she pulled out the cutting board to cut up the chicken breast for the salad.

Lotrel walked up behind his wife while she stood at the kitchen counter. He wrapped his arms around her waist. "Hey babe," he said as her kissed her cheek.

"Hey baby, how do you like my hair?" she asked, turning around so her husband could see her new look.

"Shit, I'm loving the new look. It's like I got another woman in the house. How much did we have to pay for you and the girls to get all dolled up?" Lotrel asked.

"$700," Jewel said, not thinking anything about it.

"Seven hundred damn dollars Jewel?" Lotrel asked, not wanting to believe that his wife wasted all that money on braids.

"Lotrel Turner last time I can recall I do work a full-time job, and I don't overspend like you do most of the time. This hairdo will last me a couple of months, so stop crying about what I spent," Jewel said, not wanting to discuss the issue.

"Well I'm going to say something when you drop hundreds of dollars on getting you and the girls' hair done. That's a damn house or car note, Jewel. Last time I spent a large amount of money like that was when I spent $850 to go on that hunting trip. That included airfare, hotel, transportation and licenses to hunt with my homeboys," he said.

Jewel bumped Lotrel with her hip as she continued to prepare dinner for the family. "Can you go to the grocery store and buy some butter for the garlic cheese bread? We don't have any in the refrigerator," Jewel said, ignoring her husband's justification for his spending.

Lotrel didn't answer. He just grabbed his keys. "You need anything else?" he asked.

"That's it," Jewel said. Lotrel shook his head as he drove to the grocery store. He was mad about Jewel spending so much money without consulting him. When Lotrel got home, Jewel finished cooking and the family was at the table together for dinner within 15 minutes.

About The Author

Sherre Still is a woman who has stopped at nothing to fulfill her dreams of becoming an author. The Saint Louis, Missouri native has written several novels and strives to entertain and inspire with her work. She credits God for giving her the gift of writing and putting her in company with people to be on her team to help her dreams come to fruition.

Made in the USA
Middletown, DE
26 February 2019